Love, Lies & Deception

Lora Flannery-Dietel

PublishAmerica
Baltimore

© 2003 by Lora Flannery-Dietel.
All rights reserved. No part of this book may be reproduced, stored in a retrieval system, or transmitted in any form or by any means without the prior written permission of the publishers, except by a reviewer who may quote brief passages in a review to be printed in a newspaper, magazine, or journal.

First printing

ISBN: 1-4137-1286-X
PUBLISHED BY PUBLISHAMERICA, LLLP
www.publishamerica.com
Baltimore

Printed in the United States of America

This book is dedicated to
my family for their constant support,
my children for the love they have given me
and
to my husband, Fred, who told me I could do it.

In loving memory of my sister Peggy.

Love, Lies & Deception

Chapter One

It seemed like a lifetime ago, already, that Sarah's life had been changed forever. She still remembers the fear she felt like it was yesterday. Sarah had just celebrated her eighteenth birthday and was a freshman at UW Lacrosse. Home was in a small town in Minnesota. Not too far, but far enough for her to spread her wings. She was enjoying her new found freedom. An only child, her parents had kept a really tight rein on her. She was amazed they had agreed to let her go to school so far away from home. She had just finished opening her presents from them. Her mother had sent her a pair of antique pearl earrings that were her grandmothers and her father, an early edition of Moby Dick. She was amused at how different they were and it showed in their choice of gifts for her. Her mother had been a housewife her entire life and was proud of the fact her family had always come first. Her father was an insurance broker for a local firm in Minnesota, but his true passion was American Literature and encouraged Sarah to read every chance she had. There was a knock on the dorm room door. Campus security was there with the local police department.

"Were we being too loud Officer? They were just singing to me."
"No, it's nothing like that. Is there a Sarah Wellington here?"
"Yes sir, I'm Sarah Wellington."
"We have something to tell you. You may want to sit down."

They left out the horrific details, but when it was all said and done, they believed it was a burglary gone awry. Both of her parents had been viciously murdered and for what? Her parents didn't have anything of value. They never caught the person or persons responsible. Her head still swirls as she remembers the anger and fear she felt. Luckily, her parents had enough life insurance for her to finish school. The house had been in her family for generations and had long since been paid for. Both her parents were only children and suddenly she was all alone.

When the police finally left her room that night, she sat on the bed and sobbed like a baby. Why did this have a happen to me?

That felt like a life time ago already. Sarah had finished college and returned back to the house. The house that had held the key to a nightmare that would never be just a nightmare, it was her reality.

Work had become her only enjoyment. She spent the majority of her days looking at insurance claims. She was only twenty-six and should have felt like she had her whole life in front of her. Instead it felt as though she was missing it. Her friends from high school had either moved away or gotten married and had children. Her family was gone and she was all alone. At least at work she felt like she belonged.

She finished school receiving a degree in finance. She worked for two years at the local bank until the only person left in town she felt comfortable socializing with offered her a job. He was her father's oldest and dearest friend. She knew she would be comfortable there since her father had spent so many years at the same firm. She spent the next two years working her way to claims adjuster. It all happened rather quickly, but not considering her job was her life. She had spent many long days and nights on the job. Trying in the end, to escape the reality of her life.

The house had been empty for the four years while she had finished school. She would only go home on rare occasion just to make sure that nothing was vandalized.

After all that time away, the house was in desperate need of repairs. The roof was the most pressing to date. The income she made as a claims broker for the local firm was good, but not enough to keep up repairs on the house. Sarah watched out the kitchen window as the rain came down hard and fast. This old roof will never hold up if it doesn't stop soon, she thought to herself. She didn't have the money to fix it now. All she could do was watch, wait and pray.

The lightning lit up the sky to the North like the fourth of July. She noticed there were headlights off in the distance headed right for the house. It was almost midnight, who would be coming to see me at this time of night? She quickly grabbed a hammer on her way to the door and the bell rang just as she looked through the peep hole. A very large man was standing at her front door. She was frightened and sorry she hadn't purchased a gun. With everything she had been through it would have seemed logical. The loud banging of his fist against the hard oak door brought shivers down her spine.

"Open the door please, Ms. Wellington, my name is Deputy Williams."

A sheriff's deputy, here, at this time of night? It brought back a lot of bad memories of that awful night from the past. She quickly opened the door and set down the hammer.

"Is there a problem Officer?"
"I am sorry to alarm you ma'am. My name is Deputy John Williams. There was a prison breakout two nights ago and well, were not sure if the man is coming this way or not, but I wanted to warn you. We just wanted to make sure that you have all your doors and windows locked and watching out for anyone looking suspicious."
"If you ask me, you look suspicious."
"I'm sorry ma'am; I didn't mean to alarm you."
"Would you please stop calling me a ma'am?"
"Yes ma'am, I mean, yes Ms. Wellington. Would you like me to have a look around as long as I'm here?"
"If you think it will make you feel better."
The deputy could see the look of suspicion on her face as he

began to look through the house.

"Do you live here all alone?"
"Yes, are you new to the area?"
"I just transferred here from Oklahoma, why do you ask?"
"You haven't done your homework."
"Excuse me, what do you mean?"
"My parents were murdered in this house and all the local authorities know the story very well. You asked if I lived here alone. Only a stranger would ask that question. So what's the name of the prisoner that escaped?"
"I'm sorry but that's confidential."
"Confidential? Do you at least have a description of the man? I mean, who exactly am I supposed to be watching out for?"
"I'm not making a very good first impression, I can see. I can tell you that the man is 6'2", brown hair, and brown eyes and has a tattoo on his right hand. I'll just finish up here and be on my way then."
"That would be good; I would like to get some sleep tonight."
"Everything seems to be secure. No one would get into this house without you hearing them, you have it booby trapped."
"What? Oh the buckets? Just trying to catch the rain that's coming in."
"How's it getting in?"
"The roof is leaking."
"You really should have that fixed before you hurt yourself."
"Thank you deputy. I'll keep that in mind, goodnight."
"Good night Ms. Wellington."

John jumped back in his truck and headed back for the hotel. I can't believe how beautiful she is, he thought to himself. I have to find a way to protect her.

Sarah had a hard time falling asleep. It was a little unnerving, thinking about a prisoner on the loose.

Her alarm went off at 5:30 a.m. and she felt like she had just closed her eyes. A hot shower would be sure to help. Her cell phone was ringing just as her foot hit the cold porcelain floor of the shower.

"Hello"
"Sarah, is that you?"
"Who is this?"
"It's Devon, are you okay?"
"Why wouldn't I be?"
"I heard about the prison break out on the news last night. Thinking of you in that big house alone worried me."
"I'm fine really. A sheriff's deputy was here at midnight making sure of that."

Devon was an old friend of her father's and now her boss. He always reminded Sarah of him. He was about 10 years younger than her father was when he passed and always seemed as though he was trying to shield her from harm. He is very attractive for 42 and not a grey hair on his head. Very smart, but he knew it. That was the only thing she didn't like about him. He was arrogant.

"What did he have to say?"
"You caught me getting in the shower. I'll be in as soon as I finish."
"Good, we can talk then."

She arrived at the office forty-five minutes later. Devon was waiting for her with a cup of coffee in hand.

"Thank you; you don't know how badly I need this."
"No problem, now what was the name of the deputy who visited you last night? He would be a good place to start, don't you think?"
"Start what?"
"Aren't you the at least a little bit curious about who escaped?" Devon asked in amazement.
"I guess so. His name was Deputy John Williams."

Devon felt himself begin to panic as the name came out of Sarah's mouth. He had to think and think fast. What was he doing here and what did he want?

"That doesn't sound familiar."

"He said he had just transferred here from Oklahoma. I'm going to call the department and see what he can tell me today, if anything about the prisoner who escaped."

"Let me know what they tell you."

"Don't worry, I will."

After a call to the local sheriff's department, Sarah walked into Devon's office with a dazed look on her face.

"What's wrong, Sarah? Did you get any more information from our friendly deputy?"

"Devon, they have never heard of a deputy John Williams."

"What in the world are you talking about? Maybe you got his name wrong."

Devon couldn't help but smile to himself. Sarah won't want anything to do with him now.

"No, I don't believe I did. If that wasn't a real deputy at my house last night, then who was it? I can't believe I let him into my house without seeing his badge, what was I thinking?"

"You obviously weren't thinking Sarah! You're lucky you aren't the headline story this morning. WOMAN FOUND DEAD IN HOME."

"Did you hear the name of who escaped?"

"No, they didn't release it."

"When I asked the deputy last night for the name, he said it was confidential."

"Confidential, that would be a matter of public record."

"I know, and I don't think he wanted me to know the name. Do you think this could have anything to do with my parents' murder?"

"Sarah, you're jumping to conclusions now."

"I don't know what else to think."

"How could it possibly have anything to do with your parents?"

"Devon, I think we have more than a prison break out on our hands. I think we need to find out what we can. There is definitely something going on here but something tells me that it's more than just someone escaping from prison."

After making a few more calls, Sarah was anxious and ready to go home. Nothing more could be done today. No one was releasing any information. The house seemed even emptier tonight than usual. Being alone hadn't bothered her in a long time. She had since gotten over that. Tonight, it seemed to consume her every thought. After a good night's sleep, she would feel better in the morning.

Sarah awoke to warm sunlight hitting her face. The rain had finally stopped and she was grateful. She had forgotten about the roof with everything else going on. She had to gather her thoughts and remember what she could about her mysterious visitor. Who was he and what did he want from her? Maybe he was trying to tell her something, but what?

Sarah let the hot water from the shower run down her long lean back. She tried to remember what she could about the visitor. It was dark and with the rain he had on a dark rain coat with a hood. She remembered his eyes though. They were a deep blue, almost the color of the sky before a storm. Now that she thought about it, they had a mysterious look of concern in them. It seemed odd now knowing what she knew, or for that matter, didn't know. Who was he and why did he appear so concerned for her safety?

The water quickly turned cold and it only reminded Sarah of something else that needed replacing in the old house. She quickly stepped out of the shower, dried off and got dressed.

It was a chilly morning, even with the sunlight. She was glad now that she had purchased a black car. It always felt so warm getting into when the sun was shining. She was anxious to get into the office to get back to finding out who escaped and more important, who John Williams was.

Her train of thought was interrupted by the ringing of her cell phone.

"Hello."
"Hello, Ms. Wellington?"
"Who is calling please?"
"This is Deputy Williams from last night."

Her head began to race with confusion. She had to find out what she could without letting on that she knew he wasn't who he said he was. He obviously knew something about who had escaped though and she needed to find out what.

"Yes, I remember. What can I do for you?"
"I was just calling to find out if you have seen anything unusual or suspicious?"
"Like our 6'2" friend with brown hair, brown eyes and a tattoo?"
"Yes, I guess, for starters."
"No, but I have to admit I haven't been on the look out either. Can you tell me who escaped yet?"
"Sorry, I can't release any information at this time. You need to be cautious!"

Sarah could feel her self getting more irritated by the moment. Who was this guy and what did he want with her?

"I'm always cautious. By the way, when did the sheriff's department start going out warning people?"
"When we deem it necessary."
"Well, if I see anything unusual is there a number where I can reach you?"

"I can give you my cell phone number. I'm on the road a lot, undercover as of sorts."

"You don't say, that must be exciting!"

Sarah knew she had to play his game, at least for now.

"It can also make it very difficult to make new friends. Well, don't be afraid to call me if you need anything. The number is....."

"Never mind, I just realized it showed up on my phone when you called. I'll just jot it down from that, thanks. I'll call if anything comes up."

She couldn't wait to call Devon; he wasn't going to believe this.

"Devon, it's Sarah."

"What's up? Did you remember anything about your mystery deputy?"

"I just hung up with him."

"What?"

"You heard me; I just hung up with him."

"What did he say? What did he want?"

"We can talk about it tomorrow."

"Sarah, be careful."

"Don't worry Devon; you should see what I can do with a hammer."

"What?"

"Never mind. I'll see you tomorrow."

Sarah was a little nervous and surprisingly enough, hungry. She sat down and ate a salad. Her stomach wasn't able to handle much, it was jumpy from nerves. It was easier to try and sleep, if only her mind would let her.

She woke up the next morning and still felt very ill at ease. At least at work she had something else to think about. Sarah went to

Devon's office the next morning and sat down.

"Devon, please stop pacing and sit down."
"Close the door; there are too many ears around here."
"Devon, you are way too dramatic."
"Sarah, until we know what's going on, we need to be careful. So what did Mr. Williams have to say?"
"He played it off like he was concerned for my safety, asking if I had seen anyone unusual hanging around."
"Well, have you?"
"Devon, please, what would this prison escape have to do with me? Maybe this man just has some sort of sick infatuation with me, and is using it as an excuse for hanging around."
"We really don't know, do we? You need to be careful, my dear. I think you should stay with me for a little while. At least until we find out what's really going on?"
"You're joking, right? Can you imagine the scandal and the office gossip?"
"I really don't see how that matters now. Your safety is more important than anything."
"I'll think about it, but right now we need to put our heads together and find out what we can about either Mr. Williams or the man who escaped. One or both of them hold the key to this mystery."
"Fine, but if this gets any stranger, I won't take no for an answer from you young lady!"
"Okay, now I think we should start over in Oklahoma. Maybe that part of his story was true."
"I wouldn't count on it."
"Do you have a better idea?"
"No, but while you do that, I think I should find out whatever I can about who escaped."
"Good, it sounds like we should probably talk again later."
After a few minutes on the phone Sarah realized she had an ally at the sheriff's department. An old high school class mate of hers named Susan was the secretary to the Sheriff and was more than

willing to tell Sarah what she knew. A man had escaped from a prison two towns north of where Sarah lived and his where about were still unknown. She couldn't tell her what his name was though, that information was not available. Susan thought that was strange, but wasn't going to tell Sarah that.

Sarah met back up with Devon to let him in on what she had learned. She opened the door to what seemed to be a very heated conversation. The look on his face and the flinging of his hands told her she had better get out, now! She was intrigued to find out what had him so angry, but wasn't about to walk in his office again.

The drive home relaxed her. Her mind wandered and for a few moments she forgot where she was and how she got there. When she pulled into her long driveway, a car was parked up at the house. As soon as she got close enough to see his eyes, she knew it was John Williams. She couldn't mistake those eyes anywhere. She stepped slowly out of the car.

"Hello Ms. Williams."
"Hello Deputy, what brings you out here again?"
"Well, I know this is going to sound strange, but hear me out. I have a couple of week's vacation coming and I know how bad your roof is. Well, I thought maybe you could use my help. I'm really handy and it would only cost you for the supplies and maybe dinner for my labor."
"Can I think about it?"
"Sure, but my vacation starts tomorrow, so don't wait too long."
"I won't, can I call you later?"
"Yeah, you have the number, right?"
"Yes, I have the number and I'll call you later."

Sarah turned slowly and walked up the steps to the house. Those eyes, she could feel them up and down as she walked in the house and quickly stopped and locked the door behind her. She didn't dare look back; she was too afraid.

The phone was ringing as she turned around and she was glad. If he was still out there, at least she could tell someone.

"Hello."
"Hello Sarah, I'm sorry for shooing you out of the office before."
"Devon what's wrong? You sounded quite angry with whomever you were talking to."
"Oh that was nothing really; I just wanted to say I was sorry."
"Devon, he was here when I got home tonight."

Sarah glanced through the curtain making sure that John had really left.

"Who was there?"
"Our Mr. Williams, he just left."
"Sarah, this is starting to make me very nervous. What did he want?"
"He said he had some vacation time coming and offered to fix my roof."
"You're not considering letting him do it, are you?"
"Well, it's a way of keeping him near until we find out who he really is."
"You're nuts, Sarah, absolutely nuts!"
"You're probably right, but I need to find out who he really is."
"Please reconsider Sarah, I don't like this."
"Devon, I'll be fine."
"Yeah, sure you will. You always say that."
"I'm always right, aren't I? I'll talk to you tomorrow."
"Fine, tomorrow then."

Devon put down the phone and didn't know which direction to go first. What could Mr. Williams be up to? I have to get him out of Sarah's life. I can't afford to have him around and either can she; she just doesn't know it yet.

Devon is right, I have to be crazy to consider letting him near me.

I don't know any other way to keep him close until I find out who he really is. Now, where did I put his number?

"Deputy Williams, it's Ms. Wellington, I decided to take you up on your offer."

"Great, but you will have to call me John, enough of this Deputy Williams stuff, I'm on vacation now."

"When should I expect you then?"

"How about first thing tomorrow morning?"

"If you say so, but not too early, right? As I'm sure you know I haven't been getting a lot of sleep."

"How's 8:00?"

"Fine and I'll see you then."

John found himself day dreaming about Sarah. She is so charming and beautiful. He couldn't wait to see her again. He had to remember that he was there to protect her, but tomorrow wouldn't come soon enough for him.

Chapter Two

"Morning, John."

"Good morning Ms. Wellington."

"Okay, if I have to call you John, then you have to call me Sarah."

"Good morning Sarah."

"That's much better. Where do you think we should start?"

"I'd like to take a look around inside if that's all right? It will help me decide."

"Come on in then; do you want some coffee?"

"I would love a cup."

Sarah poured his coffee and she watched him closely. He mulled around the house, looking curiously at beams and banging on walls. He was a good pretender if nothing else. He finally reached the kitchen with a look of despair on his face.

"Oh, I don't like the look on your face, what's wrong?"

"I'm afraid the roof has been leaking for quite some time now. Some of the walls are rotted and should be replaced along with the roof."

"How much money are we talking about?"

"Well, parts shouldn't be too bad, but the labor—at least two dinners instead of one."

"Why are you so willing to help me?"

"I have the time and I enjoy fixing things. Besides, I don't ever get a home cooked meal and this way I have two coming."

"You just appeared out of nowhere though."

"I think of it more as fate. I'll be back in a couple of hours."

"Where are you going?"

"I need to pick up some supplies so I can get started. It's a bigger job than I anticipated and I only have two weeks."

She tried to keep her mind occupied. Emptying all the buckets was a good place to start. She also needed to call Devon before John got back. She wanted someone to know she was alone with him.

"Devon, it's Sarah, I decided to let John fix my roof."

"Oh it's John now?"

"Devon, I have to keep him close and find out what I can."

"You need to have your head examined. By the way, I forgot to ask, did you find out anything about who escaped?"

"Yes, an old high school friend of mine is the sheriff's new secretary. A man had escaped but she couldn't tell me what his name was. She told me she would call if she could find out anything else."

"Maybe this Mr. Williams is the man who escaped?"

"I never thought of that."

"Sarah, please be careful."

"I will, don't worry."

It was almost 11:00 before John returned from the store.

"Can I do anything to help?"

"You may want to take a look around the attic and take out anything you think you might want or is still any good. The roof is going to take a few days, so it will give you time to go through it."

"I suppose you're right. I guess I'll take a look around and see what I can salvage."

Come on, Sarah, you can do it. The old stairs creaked with every step she took. Sarah wanted to turn around and forget all about the attic. You're not ten anymore, Sarah, there is nothing in the attic to be afraid of. It felt as though the door at the top of stairs got further away with each step. When she finally grabbed for the handle, it felt like ice in her fingers. She quickly turned the knob before she could change her mind. She peered around hiding behind the door, as if the boogie man was waiting to jump out at her. Pull yourself together. With one quick motion she pushed the door open.

The smell of must and mold was almost overpowering. She walked slowly to the window watching every step she took. She knew that the boards weren't very stable before and the rain certainly wouldn't have helped. She had no idea how long they were being weakened by the elements. She finally reached the window and raised it quickly as she gasped for air. She couldn't even begin to look around until she got some fresh air in there. She found an old chest and moved it just in front of the window so she could sit and wait and catch her breath.

Glancing out the window she watched John as he unloaded the lumber from the back of his pickup truck. She never realized how strong he was before. He lifted the boards from the bed with what seemed like no effort at all. His blonde hair seemed to dance in the breeze and sunlight. She realized that first night that he was much taller than her 5'6" frame. She just never realized before how handsome he was.

Getting her mind back on the task at hand, she glanced around the room. It was much smaller than she remembered. She could see that the floor boards were damp and the ceiling and walls were covered in mildew. Trying to cover her mouth as she glanced around the room, something didn't seem right. There were only a few boxes scattered throughout and they didn't seem to be in any particular order. Something was definitely wrong with this picture. Her mother would never have tolerated the disarray these boxes were in. Oh my God, the robbers must have been up here, too.

I wonder if they ever checked in here for finger prints. They couldn't find any on the main floor, but what if they never checked here? She needed to get the police back here, today!

She quickly jogged down the stairs and into the kitchen. Confusion filled her mind as she reached for the phone.

"Devon, it's Sarah."

"Sarah, is something wrong?"

"I'm not sure. Can you go back through the old newspaper articles about my parents' death?"

"Where are they?"

"In the filing cabinet next to my desk."

What are you looking for? What's happened, Sarah?

"I need the name of the investigating officer."

"Why? Tell me what's going on!"

"Devon, please just hurry and get me the name, please."

"I'll look it up and call you back as soon as I find it."

"Just hurry, okay?"

"I'll go as fast as I can. Are you sure you don't want to tell me what's going on?"

"I might be over reacting, just hurry."

What is that girl up to? Why is she suddenly asking questions again? I bet Mr. Williams is behind this some how.

Sarah heard a loud bang just as she hung up the phone. She about jumped right out of her skin. She raced for the front door and flung it open in fear.

"John, are you all right?"

"I'm fine, a board just slipped out of my hand. Why are you so jumpy?"

"You just scared me, that's all. I didn't want to find you flat on your back somewhere from falling. I don't have enough insurance for that."

"Your concern overwhelms me!"

"I wouldn't have run if I wasn't concerned. Are you really okay?"

"Yes, I'm fine. Do you want to go grab some lunch?"

"How about if I just make us lunch?"

"If it's not too much trouble that would be great."

"No, it's not any trouble at all. Is tuna fish okay?"

"Sounds good."

"Give me ten minutes and come on into the kitchen."

John and Sarah sat down for lunch. They chatted and before either of them knew it, an hour and a half had passed. The conversation flowed very easily between them, just like they were old friends. Sarah had to remember that he wasn't her friend.

"Thanks for lunch; I'd better get back to work now. There aren't many hours of daylight left."
"You're right, when did you want your 'thank you dinners'?"
"Maybe one next weekend and the other when I'm done."
"I really feel guilty, this isn't going to be an easy job and I would like to pay you something."
"Your company is payment enough, really. Besides, I enjoy doing the work. I'm going to head outside and get to work. I have something I need to take care of this afternoon, so as soon as I finish unloading the truck I'm going to have to leave."
"Okay. I'll see you tomorrow then?"
"You sure will."

She realized in all the conversation they had, she never asked him anything about his past. Hopefully tomorrow she could find a way to ask him some questions without appearing like she was prying. She also realized she had never heard back from Devon. What could be taking him so long? He knew how badly she wanted the information, why would he be hesitating so?

"Devon, what did you find out?"
"Sarah, the supervising officer was Deputy Wilkes."
"Oh God, that's great, no wonder it took you so long to call me back."
"I think I should go with you if you plan on asking him any questions."
"I wouldn't dream of asking him any questions in person. I'm not an idiot. That man has a way of trying to cop a feel every time I'm around him and he gives me the creeps. I wonder why he is listed as the investigating officer."

"I don't know Sarah; he probably had himself assigned to it so if you ever had any questions he would have to be the one to talk to you. If he gives you any problems or wants to see you in person, you call me. Do you understand me?"

"Yes Devon, I'll call if I need a guardian."

"Very funny."

"I'll talk to you later Devon."

Sarah's voice began to quiver as the phone rang on the other end.

"Sheriff's Department, Deputy Hansen speaking."

"Deputy Hansen this is Sarah Wellington. May I please speak with Deputy Wilkes, please?"

"I'm sorry, but Deputy Wilkes isn't available until Monday morning."

"Would you mind calling him at home?"

"It's bow hunting season and I'll never find him this weekend. Is there something I could maybe help you with?"

"That would be wonderful. I'm looking for some information regarding my parents' murder investigation. Do you think you could help me?"

"Wish I could, but those files are locked in Sheriff Johnson's office. I will leave a message for Deputy Wilkes to call you on Monday though. That's really the best I can do."

"Thank you, deputy."

The waiting was getting more and more irritating. She also knew John was going to think it was strange that she hadn't started to clean out the attic. She would have to make up an excuse why she couldn't do it. It was almost impossible not to get tangled up in all the deceit. She didn't want to slip up, but knew the longer she didn't let on, the harder it was going to get to keep a straight face with him. Tomorrow was another day and she would worry about it then.

Chapter Three

Sarah woke to foot steps over head. She turned to get a glimpse at the alarm clock which was flashing 12:00. The sound of a hammer slamming nails through wood rang through her ears. She flew to the window and through the down pour of rain, spotted John's truck. She threw on her robe and ran out the front door into the rain.

"John, what are you doing up there?"
"I have to get the roof covered in plastic before it comes down on top of you."
"I'll be right up to help you."
"No Sarah, it's too windy. I will only be a few more minutes. You stay on the ground."
"Be careful then and come inside when you're finished."

She needed to get dressed before John was finished covering the roof and get some coffee started, he was going to be soaked. Sarah heard the front door shut and she yelled for John.

"Grab a towel out the hall closet and there's fresh coffee in the kitchen."
"Thanks, it's really coming down out there."
"What time it is? The power must have gone out sometime last night."
"You mean you didn't hear the storm?"
"I didn't hear anything. Remember that sleep has not been high

on my priority list lately. I guess I finally slept for a change."

"That's good news. I got woke up by the storm and as soon as the lightening quit I came over. By the way it is 9:30 already."

"I can't believe I slept that late. I guess with all the rain, no work for you today?"

"I can't work outside, but I could help you with the attic if you want?"

"No, I need to get an allergy shot before I can go back up there."

"I could bring a few boxes down at a time for you to go through."

"Thanks, John, but they have mildew all over them and my allergies can't handle it. I would spend the whole day sneezing. I will be able to handle it better after my allergy shot on Monday."

"Are you sure?"

"Yeah, really, Monday would be better."

"Okay then, I guess I'll head home if you don't need my help inside today."

"Why don't you at least wait until you dry off a little? You are still soaked. I could make us some breakfast? I make a mean piece of toast."

"How about I make us breakfast?"

"I can't let you do that."

"Why not, don't you think I can cook?"

"No, it's just that you've done so much already and it hardly seems fair."

"Oh, sit down, and let the master take over!"

"Now you're the master?"

"Where do you keep the pans, you pain in the ass?"

"In the cupboard next to the stove."

"Do you like omelets?"

"Love them; what do you want to put in it?"

"Just sit down, and I'll find what I need."

Sarah sat back as John danced his way around the kitchen. It seemed so comfortable having him here. She needed to get some answers from him before she got too attached to him.

"So John, what part of Oklahoma are you from?"
"Hugo, why do you ask?"
"Just trying to get to know you, is that a problem?"
"No, but I left my past in Hugo and I'd like to leave it there."
"What about your family?"
"What about them?"
"Do you have any?"
"Nobody I care to think or talk about."
"Boy, touchy subject. Is there anything you would like to share with me?"
"I'm hungry, how about we eat?"
"I take it, that's a no?"
"Do you want some more coffee?"
"You certainly have a way of sidestepping questions you don't want to answer."

This man was very irritating and very handsome. She couldn't trust him though and she needed to remember that. He had just made that more obvious. He was hiding something about his past. Not wanting to share any part of it with her made her even more leery of him.

"The omelet was wonderful, thanks so much John."
"You're welcome. Now I'll wash if you dry."
"John, I think you've done enough already, can I clean up?"
"I don't mind really. I don't have anything else going on today."
"It's a Sunday in the middle of October. You have to watch football don't you?"
"I don't have to watch it!"
"Well I do. I have to watch Green Bay play anyway."
"Green Bay, aren't we in Minnesota?"
"Yes, but I spent four years at college in Wisconsin with a dorm full of Green Bay fans. I really didn't have a choice. They converted me."
"Is that where you were when your parents were murdered?"

"Yes, and I still feel guilty about that. Maybe if I had been home I could have done something to prevent it."
"I highly doubt that."
"Why do you say that?"
"Because whoever robbed your house wouldn't have stopped at your parents, they would have killed you too."
"I suppose you're right."
"Do you mind if I stay and watch the game with you?"
"I'd like that, it gets kind of lonely cheering all by myself."
"Oh, make no mistake; you'll still be cheering by yourself. I'm not a Green Bay fan."
"Oh, very funny."
"Let's get these dishes done so you can watch your team make fools of themselves."
"You can keep dreaming."

They finished just in time to catch the opening kickoff. Sarah wasn't exactly concentrating on the game though. She found herself attracted to John. They sat on the couch together and she had an uncontrollable urge to be held by him. She knew that wasn't an option though. She knew she needed to get away from him before she couldn't resist anymore. It all seemed kind of foolish since she didn't know what he wanted with her? She was sure it wasn't a romantic involvement though. He had gone to great lengths to get into her life though. She just wasn't sure how she could find out anything about him, or what he was doing there. He wasn't ready to open up to her yet. She would have to bide her time where he was concerned.

Chapter Four

The game seemed like it flew by. Green Bay had beaten Tampa Bay 31-7. She was more than happy to keep reminding John what the score was. Rubbing it into him amused her.

"I know you already wasted most of your day here John, but we could go out and grab a pizza for supper if you want."
"Why don't we just order something in?"
"I am beginning to think you don't want anyone to see us public?"
"I never said that. I just enjoy spending time alone with you."
"Fine. We'll eat here then. It will give us a chance to talk."
"I'll be happy to go pick up the pizza if you want to order it?"
"Great, what do you want on it?"
"Surprise me."
"Do you know where Demarks is?"
"It's on Main Street, right?"
"That's the one, it usually only takes about twenty minutes, so if you leave now the pizza should be ready when you get there."
"I'll be back in a little while then."

Sarah spent the time John was gone thinking of questions she could ask him. Are your parents still alive? What are you doing in my life? As much as she wanted to ask what he was doing there, she knew she couldn't. The telephone was ringing and Sarah quickly picked it up.

"Hello."
"Hello Sarah."
"Who is this?"
"You mean you don't know?"
"No, now who is this?"
"I'm sorry Sarah, I guess I'll just have to keep that my little secret."
"What do you want?"
"You know, you should really be more careful who you let into your home."
"What are you talking about? Who is this?"
"I think you know what and whom I'm talking about."
"No, I don't and this conversation is over."
"Just remember what I said."

Sarah hung up the phone in a fury. She looked around the living room and was suddenly very aware of her surroundings. She quickly walked around the house and pulled down the shades and locked the doors. She was shaking uncontrollably. There was a knock at the front door and she screamed.

"Sarah, let me in. Are you okay? What's the matter? Sarah, open the door!"
"Oh John, hold me please."
"You're shaking, what happened?"
"Someone just called here."
"Who called here?"
"I don't know, a man, he wouldn't tell me his name."
"What did he say?"
"He said I should be careful who I let into my home."

Sarah slowly backed out of John's arms and looked at him for the first time with real fear in her eyes.

"Sarah, what's wrong? It's just a prank phone call. This stuff happens all the time."

"It doesn't to me. Besides, he knew my name! I think you should leave now."

"I don't want you here alone."

"I thought you said it was just a prank call."

"I said that before I knew they had called you by name."

"They could have been talking about you John."

"They were just trying to frighten you."

"Well, they succeeded."

"Don't let some lunatic push me out of your life."

"What do I really know about you John? You avoid every personal question I ask you!"

"My past isn't easy for me to talk about."

"Well, you had better find a way."

"You don't understand."

"You're right, I don't understand."

"It's not that simple. You want to hear that I grew up with loving parents in a house with a white picket fence. That's not how it happened."

"I don't care what's in your past. You can tell me anything."

"If that was only true, you will care though."

"John, please open up to me."

"Sarah, I can't, for your own good believe me, I can't!"

"What is that supposed to mean?"

"Oh please, just trust me and let it go."

"I don't think that I can John if that's even your real name."

"Of course that's my real name Sarah and you have to believe me."

"I think you need to leave. I really need some time to think."

"You're still shaking and I'm supposed to leave you here alone. Besides there is some lunatic out there harassing you."

"I don't know what to do. My boss told me I could come and stay with him for a while. I might not have a choice anymore."

"You don't have to be here alone, let me stay with you."

"That wouldn't solve anything."

"I didn't mean that I wanted to sleep with you. Well, not that I don't. I think I'm going to shut up while I'm ahead."

"That's probably a good choice."

"Sarah, look into my eyes and tell me that you're afraid of me."

"The first time I saw your eyes I thought they were so calm and warm. Even now all I can see is concern."

John pulled Sarah into his arms looked into her eyes and softly kissed her lips. He pulled back slightly only to be pulled into a second kiss, but by her this time. Their lips met for the second time with desperation, neither of them wanting it to end. She pulled away slightly and stroked his face with the back of her hand. He pulled her in again as if she was the air he needed to breathe. They had crossed a line that neither of them was sure they should have.

Chapter Five

"I think that was a mistake."

"How could it be a mistake? I've wanted to do that since the first time I saw you on that rainy night."

"John, what were you doing here that first night? I know what you told me and I also know it wasn't the truth."

"What are you talking about?"

"John, I called the Sheriff Department to talk to you and they told me they had never heard of you."

"Don't be angry with me for deceiving you. I had to know that you were okay and I knew if I just knocked on your door you wouldn't have answered it. Most likely you would have called the police."

"Tell me why I still shouldn't?"

"Because you know in your heart, I wouldn't hurt you."

"What aren't you telling me? Why did you come here that night?"

"I was hoping it wouldn't come to this, but now I can see I have to tell you the truth. I don't think I have a choice anymore. You had better sit down and get comfortable. This isn't going to be easy for me to tell you."

"Please just tell me what's going on?"

"Sarah, my father was in your house the night your parents were killed."

"What are you talking about John? What do you mean your father was here?"

"My father was one of the men who robbed your house."

"What did you say?"

"Sarah, I know this isn't easy for you to hear, but you need to let me explain."

"You mean your father killed my parents?"

"No Sarah, he didn't."

"Then who did?"

"I don't know for sure, I mean, I don't have any proof."

"I can't believe what you're telling me. This is awful."

"I can explain, please just listen to me. My dad came home after he was supposed to have been out with a buddy. He had been shot in the back. He had lost a lot of blood and didn't have a lot of strength. He told me that he had been involved in a robbery and something had gone terribly wrong."

"Yes, he killed my parents!"

"He was dying Sarah and he knew it. There was no reason for him not to tell me the truth."

"Did he tell you who did kill them then?"

"I'm getting to that. Just let me explain. I need you to understand that my dad wasn't a bad man."

"How am I supposed to believe that?"

"He wanted people to know the truth."

"What is the truth, John? It was an accident that my parents were murdered?"

"No, who was actually responsible for your parents' death and why he was even involved. The only reason my father agreed to help was because he needed the money."

"Money, what money?"

"The money he was promised if he helped rob your home. My mother had cancer and my dad had lost his job when the factory he worked at closed down. She needed treatments and he couldn't pay for them anymore. They lost their insurance and she would have died without the treatments."

"That doesn't make any sense John. My parents didn't have anything worth that much money."

"Well according to my father, this man had promised him two hundred thousand dollars for his help. It was supposed to be a simple job and no one was supposed to get hurt. When the news hit about a couple being murdered and that the authorities had assumed it was a robbery gone badly, I put two and two together. I believe the man who killed your parents was Pete Swans. I should have known you would have figured out that I wasn't who I said I was. I lied to you because I thought it was best."

"Why haven't you gone to the police with what you know?"

"I have no proof, only the words of a dying man. Besides they would have thought my dad had acted alone and they would have never investigated any further."

"You could have made them listen to you."

"Sarah, I have been keeping track of Pete Swans since the night my dad died in my arms. Watching and waiting for him to slip up and give me the evidence I needed to turn him into the police."

"I can't believe how bizarre this all sounds. It just seems so unreal."

"I know it does Sarah. I will understand if, when this is over, you never want to see me again. Right now you need to let me finish. I followed him for months. I needed to know for sure what had happened. Why my father had been shot. The only thing I'm sure of is that Pete Swans is a dangerous man. I never saw fear in my father's eyes until that night. I guess it could have been the fear of dying, but I don't think so. About six months ago I was watching Swans at a local bar when he approached me. I didn't know for sure if he knew who I was at the time, but he knew I had been following him. He said if I didn't stay away from him he would kill me. He must have put two and two together and realized who my father was. I denied it, but he didn't buy it. From then on I had to keep my distance, but I was obsessed. I wanted him punished for killing your parents and my father. I was waiting for him one night outside the bar. I told him that I wasn't hiding anymore. That I would find the evidence I needed. He laughed in my face and asked what I remembered about the news coverage of the murder. I didn't understand what he was talking about. Then he looked at me with a look of contempt and muttered a single word, 'Sarah'. I tried to act like I didn't know what he was talking about but he saw through that. He laughed and said I was just like my father, a sympathetic fool. If I told anyone what I knew he would come after you. That's when I knew that I needed to find you. He wasn't going to hurt anyone else. About six weeks ago he killed someone driving drunk. They threw the book at him. I thought it was finally over; at least he was in prison. Then last week he escaped."

"We need to go to the police John."

"He wouldn't be stupid enough to show up here Sarah. Especially since the police are looking for him."

"Do you think he is the one who called here?"

"I wish I knew for sure. It would make sense though. He was trying to frighten you into getting rid of me."

"John, I'm afraid what if he comes after me?"

"I'm here Sarah and I'm not leaving you."

"You can't stay with me every minute of every day."

"No, but I can be with you as much as possible. We have to be careful that's all."

"Is it Pete Swans you described to me that first night?"

"Yes, I couldn't tell you who I was, but I needed you to be on the look out for Pete Swans."

"What do you think we should do now?"

"We keep this between us; he can't know that you know anything."

"John, if he knows you're here, he's going to know that I know the whole story."

"I don't think he knows for sure that I'm here. I just think he is trying to scare you so if I decided to show up you wouldn't want anything to do with me."

"Why did they pick my family to do this to?"

"They were after the money."

"John, I told you before, my parents didn't have a lot of money. They had just enough life insurance for me to finish school, that's it."

"Then something isn't adding up. If Pete Swans had promised my father all that money for helping him, he must have thought there was something really valuable here."

"Can you think of where they would have gotten the idea that your parents had a lot of money?"

"I have no idea John. My mother never had fancy jewelry and the only vises my father had were his books."

"Well, from what my father said, Pete Swans was working for someone else. He wasn't the brains behind the operation. They were supposed to get in and get out. My father told me that your father had caught them in the house and told them they would never find what they were looking for. I just realized, maybe my father assumed it was money."

"I don't want to hear about this."

"I'm sorry Sarah. I wasn't thinking about your feelings. I am just so bent on getting to the truth. I'm so, so sorry."

"I am angry and confused and this is too much for me to fathom."

"I understand and I'm sorry that I brought this all on you."

"I think I need to get some sleep John."

"I don't want to leave you here alone."

"I'll be fine, you said yourself he wouldn't dare show up here with the police looking for him."

"Promise me that if you hear anything unusual you'll call the police and then me."

"I will I promise. I'll talk to you tomorrow."

"Make sure you lock the door as soon as I leave."

"I will John, goodnight."

Sarah was glad when John had finally left. Her head was still spinning from everything he had told her. Maybe some sleep would help her put things into perspective. One thing she knew for sure is that she needed to talk to Devon. Maybe he could think of a way to help them. That would have to wait until morning though. She was too worked up to even talk to him tonight.

Chapter Six

Sarah hardly slept a wink. Her mind wouldn't slow down long enough. She needed to get to work and talk with Devon. He would know what she should do. She arrived at work a half and hour later. Devon was sitting in his office when she reached his door.

"What happened to you? You look terrible."
"Thanks for the compliment."
"I'm serious Sarah; you look like you haven't slept in days."
"I didn't get much sleep last night."
"Why not?"
"Oh, that's a really long story."
"I have nothing but time my dear. Close the door and tell me about it."

Sarah told Devon everything. She knew she probably shouldn't be getting him involved but in a way he already was.

"Sarah, are you sure you can trust this guy?"
"I think so Devon."
"I don't understand the part about the money though."
"That makes two of us."
"Your parents never told you about anything really valuable that they owned or that they had money stashed away somewhere?"
"Of course not, there was no hidden money or anything else of value for that matter."

"How can you be so sure?"

"I knew my parents; I had to use the life insurance money just so I could go to college."

"Sarah, something isn't adding up. I don't think you should be so quick to believe everything John tells you."

"That's why I told you the whole story. I need your help to find out what is really going on."

"Well for starters we need to talk to John again and go over this one more time."

"Why don't you come over tonight for supper? I'll invite John and we can go over this together."

"That sounds good. Sarah, do me a favor, don't tell anyone else about what John told you. We don't know at this point who we can trust and who we can't."

"If you think that's best Devon. I'll see you around 5:30 then?"

"I'll be there and Sarah, don't worry. We will figure this out together."

"Thanks Devon, you always have a way of making me feel better."

Devon knew he had a big problem and his name was John Williams. He had to protect Sarah no matter what the cost. He had to call Carl. He wasn't going to like this anymore than Devon did. They had to have a plan together in case John knew too much.

Sarah walked into her office and closed her door behind her. She sat down and her phone rang.

"Hello."

"Sarah, is that you?"

"John?"

"Yes it's me. I am so glad to hear your voice."

"What's wrong?"

"I'm fine really; I wanted to get into work early."

"Don't you have enough going on in your life right now without spending extra time at work?"

"It gives me something else to think about for a while."

"I know I'm just worried about you."

"John, are you still coming over to work on the roof today or is that over now that I know the truth."

"Yes, I'm still coming over to work on the roof."

"Do you want to stay for dinner?"

"Thank you."

"Don't thank me yet, you haven't eaten my cooking yet."

"No, thanks for still wanting to see me after everything I've told you. I half-expected you to never want to see me again."

"I have to admit that this whole thing is starting to take its toll on me. I thought all of this was in my past."

"I'm sorry Sarah."

"I know John, I know."

"I'll see you about 5:30 then?"

"Okay Sarah and I can't wait to see you."

"I'm looking forward to seeing you too, John."

Sarah was having a hard time concentrating on everything today. Her thoughts were consumed with John. Not only the terrible things he had told her, but the way she was beginning to feel about him. She couldn't let Devon know how she felt about John. He wouldn't understand and she wasn't sure she did either.

She left work early to make supper and maybe take a short nap. Once John and Devon met, she was sure things were going to get complicated. It would take all the spare energy she had keeping them both calm and focused.

John came in about 5:15 and she was glad. She needed a few minutes to be alone with him before Devon started his interrogation.

"John, I told my boss Devon everything today."

"What do you mean you told him everything?"

"I told him everything that you told me."

"Sarah, some of that was for your ears only. I think we should have talked about it first."

"I needed to talk about it with someone I trusted."

"I thought we worked through that yesterday?"

"You have to admit you dropped a really large bomb on me?"

"I'm sorry and I wouldn't have ever told you any of it if Pete Swans hadn't scared me into thinking he might hurt you."

"Let's not argue John, that's not going to solve anything."

"I'm sorry, but I'm just not sure you telling this to your boss was the right thing to do."

"Well, it's done now so let's make the best of it. He'll be here in ten minutes."

"Oh wonderful!"

"John, I just thought he could help. He has a sharp mind and a clear way of looking at things. He should be able to help us nail that asshole Pete Swans. I want him to suffer for what he did."

"So do I Sarah, but we could have handled it ourselves."

"John, I'm scared and I know that Devon will look out for me, he always has."

"If you're sure he can help us then I have to trust you."

"Knock, knock, anyone home?"

"Come on in Devon were in the kitchen."

"What smells so good?"

"I had just enough time to throw in a pot roast, I hope it's good."

"This must be John?"

"I'm sorry, yes Devon this is John, John this is Devon."

"So John, has Sarah told you that I've heard the ridiculous story you've told her?"

John could feel himself becoming angrier by the moment. Who does this guy think he is? He doesn't know the first thing about me and he is already judging me.

Sarah could tell by the look on his face that she had better intervene quickly or she was going to have a blow up her hands.

"Devon, that's not fair, I believe John and I think you need to give him the benefit of the doubt. At least until you hear his side of the story."

"I just want to know why he didn't come forward right away?"

"I explained all that to Sarah, she understands why I had to lie to her and that's all that matters to me!"

"Well, you're still going to have to convince me."

"I don't have to convince you of anything. What do you think? I just made up this elaborate story? What reason would I have for doing that?"

"Devon, John knows too much not to be telling the truth.

"Sarah I'm not as trusting as you are. He was probably here that night, that's how he knows what happened."

"That's not true; I didn't have anything to do with it."

"Well you know what they say 'The apple doesn't fall far from the tree'."

"Listen you asshole, I would never hurt anyone much less Sarah!"

"So you say."

"All right you two, I've heard enough. Were not getting any where with the two of you acting like this."

Sarah sat with her head hanging down. She was beginning to think it was a huge mistake telling Devon anything. They weren't going to get anything accomplished with them acting like this.

"Sarah, I'm not going to sit here while Devon insults me."

"Fine, then Sarah will come stay with me, we'll call the police and she can get on with her life."

"Do you idiots think you could knock it off? This is really getting annoying."

Sarah looked at both of them with contempt in her eyes. She was becoming angrier with Devon by the minute. He wasn't helping the situation. If he really cared about her, he would want to help her.

"Devon, that's not for you to decide; I need John's help."

"Did you hear that? I don't think we need your help Devon! I don't understand why you're involved anyway."

"Would you two quit it please? You both seem to forget that I'm the one that's in danger. I could really use your help. I really don't want Pete Swans getting away with what he did. Can we please just go over this together?"

"If you think you can get Devon to shut up long enough."

"Did you hear her; she wants us to get along."

"I heard her all right; do you think you could listen to me and stop judging me?"

"Fine, then let's bury the hatchet and get to the bottom of this. Now according to Sarah your father told you that Pete Swans had promised him two hundred thousand dollars for his help."

"Yes, that's right."

"Did your father every say how he was supposed to be paid?"

"No."

"Did he tell you what they were supposed to be stealing?"

"No, I just assumed that it was money."

"Why would you assume that?"

"He said it was money he was promised."

"Did it ever occur to you that Pete Swans knew your father was desperate? Played with his emotions and tricked him into helping him?"

"I guess so, my dad wasn't thinking really clearly then. What if they weren't after cash but something worth a lot of money?"

"My parents didn't have anything that valuable John."

"Did your dad tell you if Swans actually stole anything that night?"

"I don't think so."

"Why do you say that?"

"Sarah, are you sure you can handle this? Maybe Devon and I should talk alone."

"I'm all right and I can handle it. You guys aren't leaving me out of this."

"Are you sure?"

"Yes, let's just get through this; tell him what you know John."

"My dad said that Sarah's father had told Pete Swans he would never find what he was looking for. I think Swans got angry, lost his cool and well, you know the rest."

"Why did your dad think that Pete Swans was working for someone?"

"I don't think Swans had the brains to do something like this, but I really don't know for sure."

"You don't know much do you?"

John could feel himself about to lose his temper again. This guy doesn't care about finding out what really happened he just wants center stage.

"Why do you keep doing that?"
"What am I doing? I'm just trying to find out the truth."
"No you're not; you're just trying to impress Sarah."
"You're crazy; I don't have to impress Sarah she knows how I feel about her."

I can't believe Sarah is buying this, John thought to himself. He isn't fooling me; he is in love with her.

Sarah couldn't believe they were doing it again. What was going on here? Devon is usually so level headed and he is acting like a spoiled child. For that matter, John isn't acting much better.

"You know what? I want you both to leave."
"Sarah, I'm sorry, I promise I won't say another word."
"That's great Devon, but it's too late. I don't think either one of you care at all about me."

John couldn't believe that he was pulling this on her. Suddenly he was acting like the concerned friend again. There was something about him that John didn't like, but for Sarah he would at least pretend that he did.

"I'll behave Sarah, I promise."
"Lets just eat; do the two of you think we can do that? I could

really use a break."
"Now that you mention it, I've had enough of this for a while."
"John?"
"Yeah, me too, let's eat."
"Well I'm glad you guys can finally agree on something."

As the three of them sat around her kitchen table and ate, Sarah fell deep into thought. Maybe getting Devon involved wasn't the right thing to do. John was the only link to why her parents had died and she needed him. She knew that wasn't the only reason she needed him, she was falling in love with him. Devon would think she had lost her mind. She couldn't let onto him that she had feelings for John. Devon would never be able to understand that. They finished eating without any more blowups. Both John and Devon knew she wouldn't stand for it any longer.

"Do you two think we can continue without you both acting like children?"
"Yes we can, right John?"
"Go ahead; I'll do anything I can to help her find the truth."
"Did you ever see Swans meeting with anyone?"
"No."
"Never anyone on more than one occasion?"
"No, I don't think so."
"I thought you said you watched him?"
"I did, I watched him—not every person he spoke to."
"Did it ever occur to you that one of those people he talked to could have been behind this whole thing?"
"I don't think so."
"Why not?"
"He knew I was watching him. He wasn't about to give me anything I could use against him."

Sarah sat on the couch as John and Devon searched for answers. She wanted to call it a night, but was grateful that they finally seemed to be trying to work together. She suddenly felt very lucky. Something she hadn't felt in a long, long time. There were people around who cared about her.

"Sarah, are you all right?"
"Sure John, why?"
"You seem like you're in another world."
"I'm just thinking."
"I think we should call it a night."
"I think were going to have to. It's almost midnight and I can't keep my eyes open any longer."
"Well, I guess I'll see you tomorrow at work Sarah. Are we going to talk again together soon?"
"Yes, maybe tomorrow night."

Devon looked at John with contempt in his eyes.

"Are you coming?"
"I think I'm going to stay and help Sarah clean up."
"Is that okay with you Sarah?"
"It's fine Devon. I'll see you in the morning."

Devon walked out the front door and before he could reach his car John was reaching for Sarah.

"Can I hold you tonight? I just want to hold you that's all."
"That may be what you intend, but I'm not sure that we could stop at that."
"Sarah please, I need to hold you."

John reached for her hand and slowly pulled her into the bedroom and into his arms. His hand gently touched the back of her neck and pulled her in where his lips finally met hers. He felt consumed by her. He lifted her without any effort and placed her on the bed. Sarah's heart began to pound with desire. She knew it would take everything she had to resist his touch. John slowly lifted the covers over her and wrapped his arms around her slim waist.

"You're serious, aren't you?"
"What?"
"You really just want to hold me?"
"Oh Sarah, I want so much more, but I don't want any doubt in your mind. Right now I know you don't totally believe me. When you do, then I think we should make love. So for tonight I will just hold you."
"John, I believe you."
"Sarah, please it's okay. This isn't easy for me. I don't blame you for having doubts. I can see it in your eyes and I understand, really. When this is over, we will make love and I promise you it will be worth the wait."

With that, John kissed her cheek and closed his eyes. Sarah felt safe for the first time in years as she faded off to sleep wrapped in his arms.

Chapter Seven

Sarah woke up feeling completely relaxed. It was the first time in days. She rolled over and reached for John only he wasn't there. She flew out of bed and ran toward the kitchen looking for him with desperation in her eyes.

"John, where are you?"

She yelled like she had never yelled before. When he didn't answer, she could feel herself begin to panic. She ran to the front window and saw his truck was still in the driveway. Sarah ran out the front door screaming his name.

"Hey you, what's the matter?"
"When I woke up and you weren't there I got scared."
"I'm sorry; I got up early and the weather forecaster said we had rain coming. I had to get the tarp back on the roof. Come here, you're shaking."
"John, I can't do this; it's just a false sense of security with you here. I have been alone for so long and frankly I was comfortable. Then you come along and suddenly I need you."
"What's wrong with that? I need you too!"
"I don't want to need anyone. It hurts too badly; everyone I have ever loved is gone."
"We're never going to get past this are we? You will never be able to look at me without me being a constant reminder of what my

father did to you?"

"John, that's not what I see, I'm just so afraid I'm going to lose you. When I woke up and you weren't beside me, I panicked. I needed you and I don't like needing you."

"Sarah, nothing is going to happen to me."

"John, neither of us knows what the future holds."

"I know we don't, but I'm hoping we will be together."

"I hope so too John."

"Go back inside before you catch cold out here. I'll be in, in a few minutes."

Back inside, Sarah new she had to get ready for work. She would have rather stayed at home and talked with John today. With the rain coming in he wouldn't be able to get anything done on the roof. She quickly grabbed her clothes and brought them into the bathroom with her so she would have them when she got out of the shower. She hadn't worried in a long time about anyone being around. She was use to running around naked if she wanted. For a split second she thought about leaving them in her room. It would have been interesting to see how John reacted if she walked out of the bathroom naked, but she thought better of it. Besides, now she had Swans to worry about. She needed a shower even if was only a quick one. She finished and got dressed in a hurry, before she changed her mind about shocking John. She opened the bathroom door and ran right into him.

"I'm sorry; I didn't see you standing there."

"That's okay, I didn't mind really. Hey, I have an idea, I can't work outside today, but I would be more than happy to bring down some of those boxes from the attic for you to go through when you get home. You got your allergy shot yesterday right?"

"Oh God John, I forgot all about the attic. I need to call the sheriff's department."

"What are you talking about?"

"The attic John, something isn't right about the attic."

"Sarah, you lost me."

"I know I'm talking in circles I guess I should explain. Last Sunday morning when I went into the attic to see what I could salvage something wasn't right. The boxes were all over the place and I new that my mother would have never left it like that. I think Pete Swans may have been in the attic that night. Maybe he left some evidence up there? Just one finger print and we can get him put away for the rest of his life."

"They could also find my dad's finger prints!"

"What does that matter now? We need to get Swans put away; I can't go on the rest of my life being afraid that he could be around the next corner."

"I know you're right, I just know my father didn't want to get involved in this and people will never understand. Go call the sheriff's department, maybe Swans was up there."

Sarah jumped on the phone and was unfortunate enough to get Deputy Wilkes.

"Sheriff's Department, Deputy Wilkes speaking, may I help you?"

"Deputy Wilkes, this is Sarah Wellington."

"Well hello Ms. Wellington, what can I do for you today?"

"I need you to look up the report from the night of my parents' murder."

"Now why do you need me to do that?"

"I need to know if anyone checked the attic for evidence."

"Well I'm sure we did Ms. Wellington that would have been very sloppy of us if we hadn't."

"Deputy, could you please just check the report?"

"I suppose it wouldn't hurt anything, what do you think is up there?"

"I don't know for sure, but someone was definitely up there."

"What makes you say that?"

"Oh Deputy, please just look it up and call me back, please."

"Yes I will, calm down. Do you want me to come over?"

"No, I don't want you to come over; I just want to know what the report says."

"Fine I'll look it up and call you back."

Sarah paced back and forth waiting for Deputy Wilkes to call her back.

"Are you okay, Sarah?"

"I'm just nervous; I hope the sheriff's department didn't look in the attic."

"I know Sarah, but will know soon."

Chapter Eight

Deputy Wilkes hung up the phone and knocked on Sheriff Johnson's office door.

"Excuse me Sheriff. I need the Wellington file."
"For what?"
"Sarah Wellington called wanting to know if we had checked the attic for evidence."
"Why would she want to know that?"
"She thinks there might be evidence up there that we missed in our initial investigation."
"Wilkes, I'll pull the file and call her back myself."
"It's no problem for me to call her back, besides I need an excuse to ask her out."
"Forget it and you leave that girl alone. I don't want you using this department for your personal gain. Now please close the door behind you."
"Yes sir."

Sheriff Johnson was suddenly very concerned. What is that girl up to, he thought to himself? Why would she think someone was in her attic? I guess I had better call her and find out what she's up to.

"Miss Wellington, Sheriff Johnson here."
"Sheriff, why are you calling me back?"
"I had to send Deputy Wilkes on an errand."

"Well thanks for taking the time. Did you find out anything?"

"Deputy Wilkes explained your concerns to me and let me assure you that we had checked the attic and unfortunately we didn't find anything. I think we were dealing with a pro here. Has something happened that I should be aware of?"

"No, not really I was just upstairs looking around and I thought maybe that part of the house wasn't part of the initial investigation."

"Well I wouldn't worry, I'm sure whoever was responsible is long gone."

"I'm sure you're right. Well, thanks for checking and getting back to me."

"If anything comes up that you need to talk to me about, please don't hesitate to call me."

"I will, thank you Sheriff."

Sarah hung up the phone with a look of despair on her face.

"Well, what did he say?"

"That they had checked the attic and they hadn't found any prints up there either."

"I'm sorry Sarah, but we will have to find another way."

"How John? I don't know where to begin."

"We'll figure this out together, I promise."

"I need to get to work."

"Oh play hooky and we can go through some of the boxes now."

"I can't. Devon wouldn't be happy."

"Who cares if Devon isn't happy?"

"Be nice, I know you two don't get along, but he's been good to me."

"I know. Just stay home today and spend it with me. You can take me down memory lane."

"Oh all right, you talked me into it. I'll have to call Devon after I find my sick voice."

"Hello Devon, it's Sarah."

"Sarah, are you okay? You don't sound well?"

"Just a start of a cold. I think I should just get some extra rest today and I should be fine tomorrow."

"When are we going to talk with John again?"

"Can we do that another night?"

"That's fine with me, but until I'm sure were getting straight answers out of him you be careful."

"Devon sometimes you're impossible."

"Sarah, I mean it and I don't trust him."

"I'll be careful Devon, I promise. By the way I talked to Sheriff Johnson today."

"About what?"

"I don't think I mentioned this to you, but I went into the attic on Sunday and the boxes up there were all over the place. I called the sheriff's department to make sure they had checked for prints up there too."

"What did the Sheriff say?"

"That they had, with no luck, so it was a dead end."

"I'm sorry Sarah, you get some rest today and we'll worry about all that tomorrow."

"Thanks Devon, I'll see you then."

Devon quickly hung up the phone and picked it up again just as quickly.

"May I speak with Sheriff Johnson please?"

"Can I tell him whose calling?"

"Devon Grant."

"No problem Mr. Grant, I'll put you right through."

"Well Devon, how nice to hear from you?"

"Cut the crap Carl, what are we going to do about this?"

"You need to calm down."

"I am calm, now what are we going to do about this?"

"I handled it Devon and I told her that we covered the whole house."

"She doesn't suspect anything?"

"I don't think so. She sounded satisfied on the phone."

"I knew we shouldn't have tried to pull this off. Now William's kid shows up and is going to screw up everything."

"From what you've told me he doesn't know anything about us."

"Nothing he's letting on anyway. What if he knows the real story and he tells Sarah."

"Devon, he would have told her already if he knew."

"You know Sarah as well as I do, she won't stop until she knows what happened."

"Well then, I guess we will just have to help her out."

"What do you mean?"

"She's got to have some doubt about William's kid already right?"

"I keep trying to convince her not to trust him."

"That's good, we couldn't have asked for a better solution to our problem. All we have to do is frame John for their deaths. Then he will be in prison and you can get close to her. When you do, we can remove any evidence that could be at her house."

"Are you nuts?"

"Do you want this over for good, or not?"

"Of course I do, but I'm just not sure that this is the answer."

"We don't have time to think. You're the one who was bent on protecting her from the beginning. We are in way too deep now for you to get cold feet."

"Oh sure, why didn't I think of that. We just have to frame John and then hope Sarah comes running for me."

"You don't sound like you think it will work. Who else does she confide in but you?"

"No one, but you want me to get romantically involved with her?"

"Please quit acting like that would be a problem for you. The whole town new you had eyes for that girl before she ever left for Wisconsin."

"Please, she was just a kid then."

"Well, she's not anymore. She is quite the looker now."

"Just quit talking about her like she a piece of property all right?"

"Calm down. I'm just giving you a hard time."

"I don't understand if we already searched the whole house and it wasn't there, where could her father have put it?"

"Well I forgot to mention that. We never did check the attic."

"What! You idiot, you mean there could be evidence up there?"

"I don't know, but we had better get to it before she starts snooping around up there again."

"How do you suggest we do that?"

"Devon, she trusts you, take her out to dinner, let me know when and I'll get in there and look myself."

"You had better get in and get out. I won't be able to cover for you if you get caught in there."

"You had better remember who you're talking to. Without my help, Sarah would already know the truth."

"I know and I can't believe you've come this far for me?"

"Don't forget it either. I have really put my neck out on the line for you, besides my career. If anyone ever finds out the truth, I would lose it all. Do you think you can get Sarah out of the house tonight?"

"No, she called in sick today. I can call her and ask her out to dinner tomorrow night. Why, what are you thinking?"

"If you can get her out of the house for a couple of hours. It will give me a chance to get in and see if I can find anything."

"I'll find a way to get her out of that house. No matter what it takes."

Chapter Nine

"John, don't bring too many—just a couple at a time."

"Oh don't worry I won't. They are really soggy. Where do you want me to put them?"

"Just put them on the floor."

"Be careful Sarah, they are pretty wet. The bottoms are ready to fall out."

Sarah ripped through the tape holding the box closed like it was butter. She was excited and sad all at the same time.

"Oh boy!"

"What's in it?"

"Some of my father's books; I didn't realize how hard this was going to be."

"We don't have to do this today if you don't want to."

"No, it's all right; I'm glad they are okay considering how wet the box was."

"Do you want to go to the next one?"

"Yes, could you please hand me the small one on top?"

"Here you go."

The tears welled up in her eyes as soon as she opened the box.

"Sarah, maybe we should do this another day?"

Her voice quivered as she quietly whispered to John.

"It's my parents wedding albums. They were so happy John, it just doesn't seem fair. They were in the prime of their lives. I was finally out of their hair. They finally would have had some time alone for the first time in years. I never thought of that before now. Probably because I didn't know what being in love felt like. Not their kind of love anyway."

"Sounds like they were special together."

"Oh they were. Always holding hands. People use to comment that they acted like newlyweds. Of course I was always embarrassed by it. Parents weren't supposed to be in love for crying out loud."

"I'm sorry Sarah; I wish my father had never gotten involved."

"I know, let's just keep going okay?"

"Which box do you want next?"

"Oh, it doesn't matter; whichever one you grab is fine."

"This one looks interesting."

"What makes you say that?"

"It has confidential written on the box."

"I don't remember seeing this one before. I wonder what's in it?"

"Open it and find out."

"Give it here and I will."

"Yes ma'am!"

"That's not funny, John."

"Oh sure it is; I like it when you're forceful."

"You think you're cute don't you?"

"Open the box, it has my curiosity peeked."

John was right; this box didn't look like the others. The ends were just folded between each other, which meant her mother didn't store this box. Her father must have put this one away without her mother knowing about it. As Sarah unfolded the flaps of the box top see began to sneeze. The mildew had soaked the box and she hoped what was inside was undamaged.

"Well, what's in it? I bet it's pictures of you as a kid—let me see."

"Sorry to disappoint you, it's just papers."

"What kind of papers?"

"They look like some sort of legal documents. This one is the deed to the house, I think. I wonder why my dad put them in the attic and not in the safety deposit box."

"Would you mind putting this one in my bedroom? I think I'll have a professional look over the papers and tell me what they all are."

"If you say so; aren't you at least a little bit curious though?"

"Of course, but it's a lot of legal jargon that I don't understand. I'll just get frustrated."

"You're right and I'll put it away for now."

"I will take them into an attorney tomorrow."

"Sarah, wait a minute. Didn't the Sheriff say they had checked the attic?"

"Yes, so what does that have to do with anything?"

"If they had, don't you think they would have checked the boxes?"

"Not necessarily, they just can't start opening boxes for no reason."

"Sarah, they would have had to have looked for evidence up there and I can tell you no one has been in these boxes before us. "

"What makes you say that?"

"These boxes have been sitting in water and if they had moved them they would have fallen apart."

"Why would the Sheriff tell me they were then?"

"I don't know, but I think that you shouldn't tell anyone that you found those papers."

"Where should I hide them?"

"I don't know, but you should do it alone. I don't want to know where you put it."

"What would make you say something like that?"

"I just don't want anyone to get the wrong idea."

"No one is going to think anything."

"You're right, because I won't know anything."

"Okay John. You win. I'll hide it myself."

"Can we relax a little while now?"

"I won't be able to relax until I know what these papers are and that Peter Swans is back in prison. For good this time and who else is behind this."
"Sarah, the phone is ringing."
"I wonder who that could be?"
"Hello."
"Sarah, you sound better."
"Oh, hello Devon."
"Are you feeling as good as you sound?"
"I got a couple extra hours of sleep, I feel a little better."
"Good enough to go to dinner with me tomorrow night? I would like to talk to you alone."
"About what?"
"Can we talk about it tomorrow night over dinner?"
"I guess so."
"Tomorrow night then?"
"Won't I see you tomorrow at work?"
"I'm sorry, I just wasn't thinking. I'll see you tomorrow morning."

Sarah hung up the phone and immediately felt something wasn't right about her conversation with Devon. He hadn't sounded like himself. Something in his voice made her a little nervous.

"What did he want?"
"He wants to take me out to dinner tomorrow night."
"He's going to try to convince you I'm no good!"
"You don't know that."
"Just wait and see Sarah; you know I'm right. Please just don't tell him anything. At least not until we are sure who is involved."
"I won't."
"I know you have a lot on your mind, but can we just talk for a while?"
"What do you want to talk about?"
"Us!"
"I wasn't sure there was an 'Us'."

"Sarah, when I came here, all I was trying to do was warn you. Then when I saw you, I suddenly felt a whole lot more. I knew I had to protect you and I wanted to protect you. There was something about you that I was drawn to. You were so trusting even after everything you have been through. When you figured out that I wasn't a real sheriff's deputy you still let me into your home."

"That's because I need to know what you knew and how you knew Pete Swans."

"So, me thinking that we have something real is a mistake?"

"No, I believe we do have something real. We just need to let it happen. Did you want to make love the other night?"

"Of course I did, but I just want it to be right when we do."

"I don't believe it could ever be wrong."

"I don't either, but I want to know that when we do, you will give me all of you."

"When that day comes, trust me, I will."

The moment seemed like too much for both of them. They were drawn to the warmth of each other. Neither one wanting to release the bond they had. John looked into her eyes with pure hunger. He wanted to just take her right there. He knew she probably wouldn't resist, but in the end they would probably both regret it. John couldn't live with that. He kissed her lips ever so slowly. They felt like rose petals against his. He knew at that moment that he would love her forever.

"Are you hungry?"
"Yes, but what I'm hungry for you can't fix with food."
"Well, let's see what we can find."
"I really could use a nap; going through the boxes has been more stressful than I anticipated."
"You go lay down and I'll make us some dinner."
"That's very nice of you John, but you don't have to do that."
"I know. I want to, so go lay down. Sweet dreams."
"Yeah, I only hope."

Sarah went to sleep and John was left to think alone. I hope I'm wrong and Devon isn't behind all of this. Sarah will have a hard time excepting that and she may never trust anyone again.

Chapter Ten

"Devon, it's Carl, did Sarah agree to have dinner with you?"
"Tomorrow night, I'll have her meet me right after work. That should give you a little more time."
"What about John, when does he usually go home?"
"I'm not sure, I would think by dusk. I'll ask Sarah tomorrow and let you know."
"Just make sure you do. I don't want him ending up being there and spoiling our chance. If he really doesn't know the truth, we don't want to help him out."
"I will, just wait for my call tomorrow."

Devon sat in deep thought. I can't believe we never looked in the attic in all years it had sat empty. Carl had me convinced that it wasn't there. I should have looked myself so I knew for sure. If Sarah finds out the truth after all this time she won't want anything to do with me, ever.

Sarah awoke to John standing over her. She could see the love in his eyes and she was glad he was there.

"Hey sleeping beauty, are you ready to eat?"
"Smells good, what it is?"
"Oh just something I whipped together."

They walked into the kitchen and Sarah was amazed. The table was covered in a linen table cloth she hadn't used since her mother had passed. A fresh flower arrangement sat in the middle surrounded by candle light. It looked like something out of a magazine.

"When do you have time do all this?"
"You've been sleeping for three hours now. It wasn't hard."
"Three hours! I'm so sorry, I never meant to sleep that long."
"Don't feel bad. You must have needed the rest. Besides it gave me a chance to do this right."
"I can't believe you did all this for me."
"I would do anything for you. I hope I didn't over step my bounds with the table cloth. I found it in the hall closet."
"Don't be silly, it looks great and I'm glad you found it. It reminds me of my mother. Lets eat, it smells great."
"Are you sure you're not upset about me using the table cloth?"
"No really, it's okay John."
"Sit down and I'll get it ready."
"You are spoiling me."
"Good, that's just what I wanted."
"Lasagna, I can't believe you made lasagna. That's my favorite, how did you know?"
"I didn't, I just got really lucky I guess."
"This is wonderful John. You have been so wonderful to me. I appreciate you being here for me."
"That's easy, I love being with you."

Sarah sat at the table staring at John. She couldn't believe the feelings she was having for him. He had become a very important part of her life and she was glad.

"This is wonderful."
"Thanks, I'm glad you're enjoying it."
"I'm cleaning up John and I'm not taking no for an answer."
"Okay, you win, you clean up."
"Turn on the lights or I won't be able to see anything."

John walked over and flipped on the light switch. The kitchen was immaculate. Every thing was already done except the dishes they had eaten on.

"You are such a brat; I can't believe you did all this for me."
"I ate too you know; besides I knew you would want to clean up so I beat you to the punch."
"That's not fair, tricking me into thinking I could clean up."
"You can, our dishes have to be washed."
"Very funny."
"Oh relax; I was just trying to be good to you."
"I know and I just feel bad. Besides, I'm not use to this kind of treatment."
"Don't feel bad please, and I wanted to do it for you."

She walked across the room and gently kissed him.

"You're welcome. You want to watch some TV?"
"Are you sure you don't have anywhere to be?"
"Just right here with you."

The evening went too quickly for both of them and they knew it was time for John to leave. If anyone saw his truck parked there over night people would be sure to talk. They didn't need any gossip interfering.

"I think it's time for you to go."
"Do I have to?"
"I don't want you to go either John, but I think it's best."
"Will I see you tomorrow?"
"I have to go back to work and then I have to have dinner with Devon. I probably won't see you at all tomorrow."
"I don't think I like this."
"I know, but I can't put Devon off again. I need to know what he's thinking."

"Will you call me at least?"
"Oh course, as soon as I get home tomorrow night."
"You be careful coming home alone."

They kissed goodnight and John went home. Sarah was still so tired, even after her three-hour nap. Bed sounded good and if she was sleeping she couldn't miss John.

The ride back to the hotel was a long one for John. All he could think about was Sarah and what she meant to him. Something wasn't right about Devon, but he wasn't sure what. John knew he couldn't let onto Sarah that he didn't trust Devon. She wouldn't understand and he didn't want anything coming between them.

Chapter Eleven

"Good morning Devon."

"Sarah, you look better. The day off must have been just what you needed."

"I guess so, so what did you want to talk to me about?"

"Later, okay Sarah. I'm right in the middle of a large claim. How is your roof coming along, or isn't John working on it any longer?"

"He's still working it in between helping me keep my sanity."

"How much time is he spending there every day?"

"I don't know it depends on what he's doing."

"He is going home at night, right?"

"That's kind of a personal question, don't you think?"

"I'm just worried that you might be getting too close to him."

"I'm a big girl and you don't have to worry. To answer your question, though, he's going home at night. I won't even see him today; he should be gone by the time I get home."

"Just be careful!"

"I will and I'll talk to you later."

Sarah closed the door and Devon sat back in his chair and let out a big sigh. I have to call Carl and tell him to make sure that John is gone before he sets a foot in that house. I will have to extend our dinner plans so he has time to look around.

Sarah got to her office and had a hard time concentrating. In all the years she had worked for Devon he had never asked her to dinner. It felt a little odd thinking about having a personal dinner with him alone or was it business? The day dragged along and Sarah spent most of it thinking about John. She did manage to finish a small claim she had been working on that was very sad. A van with two small children inside was hit head on and they were both killed. Their mother some how survived, but stated many times that she wished she had died too. She had a fifty thousand-dollar policy on each child and Sarah wasn't about to dispute it.

"Knock, Knock!"
"Hi Devon, are you ready to go?"
"Yeah, would you mind meeting me at Lemurs in a half an hour?"
"Of course, I'll see you then."

Sarah arrived at the restaurant and there was no sign of Devon. She asked the hostess for a quiet table in the corner. She was anxious so she ordered a glass of wine to calm her nerves. Devon arrived as she took her first sip.

"You're having wine? Sounds good, I'll think I'll have some myself. Excuse me waiter, can I get a glass of whatever she's having?"
"Yes sir, right away."
"So how are you dear? Are you holding up in all this craziness?"
"I'm fine Devon, why did you need to talk to me alone?"
"You sound angry with me?"
"Of course not, I was just curious about what you wanted to talk to me about."
"I just need to know that you're not falling for what John is telling you?"
"Excuse me sir, here is your wine. Are you ready to order?"
"No, give us a few minutes."
"Yes sir, I'll be back shortly."
"Devon, you heard the same things I did. I think John is telling the truth. I need to know why my parents were killed."
"The police never found anything to make them think it was anything, but a robbery gone badly."

"My parents didn't have anything worth taking. Why would they pick their house?"

"Robbers don't know when they pick a house what they are going to come out with. They just case a house they think they can get in and get out of without any trouble."

"What if John is right though and someone hired Swans and his father?"

"Sarah, you said it yourself. Your parents didn't have anything worth stealing. What reason would someone have to hire them to rob your house?"

"I don't know, but I'm going to find out."

"You don't even know what you are looking for."

"I know I believe John and I need to find out who is behind all this."

"Did you ever think that he just read the story about your parents' death, found out about you and now he's here seeing what he can get out of you—playing with your emotions?"

"He's not playing with my emotions!"

"What makes you so sure?"

"I know him now."

"Oh, after one week you think you know everything about him?"

"John was right, he said you would spend the whole time trying to convince me he was no good."

"I'm not trying to convince you of anything. I just want you to be careful."

"I'll be careful; it's time for me to go."

"Where are you going, we haven't even ordered yet?"

"I've lost my appetite; I'll see you in the morning."

"Sarah, I'm sorry. Don't leave just yet. Let's just sit and talk a little while. I promise I won't mention John's name again."

"I thought you were my friend! I came to you to help us figure out who was behind this. If you don't think you can do that, than John and I will figure it out on our own."

Devon knew he needed to back off or she wouldn't confide in

him any more.

"I'll help, but let's just have dinner for tonight. I think you could use a break from thinking about all that."

"I could now that you mention it. It has taken over my whole life."

"Well then, let's just have a relaxing dinner in peace."

Chapter Twelve

John was finishing cleaning up from his day on the roof. It was almost finished and then he could concentrate on putting up new dry wall inside. This meant he would have an excuse to be near Sarah, not that he needed one. He loaded up his truck and started out the driveway to head home. I guess I have to wait until tomorrow to see her. It doesn't look like she'll be home anytime soon, he thought to himself. He was halfway to his hotel room by the time he realized he had forgotten his cell phone. I can't survive without that! It gives me a good reason to go back; maybe she'll be home by time I get back there.

Sheriff Johnson pulled into Sarah's driveway and pulled his car around the back of the house. He was glad the house was a little off the beaten path. Now he could get in and out and not be noticed. He picked the lock on the back door, something he learned from one of the men that were in his custody. He always knew it would come in handy someday. He grabbed for his flashlight and made it slowly through the kitchen and headed up the stairs toward the attic. I know you're here somewhere, he thought to himself. The boxes up there had been newly opened and resealed. It was obvious by the fresh tape on each of them. Damn, she's been up here snooping around. I wonder if she found it, or if Wellington didn't hide it up here. Suddenly there was a slamming of a car door. I'm going to kill Devon, he promised me he would keep her out until at least 8:00 and it is only 6:30. Now I'm going to be stuck up here until she goes to bed.

John returned to the house and unlocked the front door. Now where did I leave that damn thing? I know, I'll just call the number on Sarah's phone, he thought to himself. He dialed the number and followed the ring into the kitchen. Turning on the light, he found it sitting on the kitchen table. As he looked to turn off the light again, he realized that the back door was open slightly. I know I locked that before I left, or at least I thought I did. I'm glad I came back now, Sarah would have freaked if she had come home to this. He quickly locked the door and headed back up the steps to the kitchen when he realized that the attic door was open too.

What is going on here, I know that door was shut when I left. Oh shit! He stopped dead in his tracks realizing someone was in the house and he feared it was Swans. Damn, I left my gun in the truck. I have to find out what Swans knows about who planned this whole thing before I call the police because once I do, he won't tell me anything. John opened the door for the attic and slowly headed up the stairs.

Sheriff Johnson was sitting still in the attic when he heard the foot steps coming up the stairs. I guess I don't have a choice anymore; I'll have to knock her unconscious so I can get out of here. The attic door opened and Carl swung his flashlight and John hit the floor. Mr. Williams, Carl thought to himself. Now what are you doing here? Oh this is too good, and I couldn't have planned this any better my self.

"Thanks for dinner Devon."
"It was my pleasure and I enjoyed spending some time with you just talking."
"I think I need to go home now and get some rest."
"Why don't you get some extra rest tonight and come in a little later tomorrow?"
"That's sweet, and I just might take you up on that offer."
"Good, I hope you do, I'll see you tomorrow."
"Good night, Devon."

The ride home was relaxing. Her dinner with Devon turned out much better than she initially expected. It was good to not have to worry for a little while about all the stuff that was going on in her life. She suddenly realized there were flashing lights on the road ahead. It didn't take long to figure out they were in front of her house. She jumped out of the car and ran to the house. Sheriff Johnson was standing in the opened doorway.

"What's going on?"
"Sarah, you need to calm down."
"As soon as you tell me what's going on."
"I was driving by and I didn't see your car around anywhere. I pulled into the driveway and saw that your attic lights were on. I decided to check it out and make sure that everything was locked up tight. I found your back door wide open, so I came in calling your name when your Mr. Williams came out of no where and waving a gun at me."
"John has my permission to be in my house. He's fixing my roof."
"He shouldn't have been waving a gun at me when I came through the door!"
"Maybe he thought you were an intruder?"
"I'm still taking him in."
"Why?"
"Because, he was waving a gun at me that isn't registered."
"You still don't have to arrest him!"
"Yes, I do, he broke the law."
"John what happened?"
"You two can talk down at the station, but right now he's coming with me."
"I'll meet you at the station John."

Sarah picked up the phone and dialed Devon as soon as they took John.

"Devon, they arrested John!"

"What are you talking about?"
"When I got home tonight, they were arresting John!"
"Who was arresting John?"
"Sheriff Johnson. You have to help me Devon. Can you meet me at the sheriff's department?"
"I'll meet you there Sarah. Calm down. We'll figure this out together."
Carl, I hope you know what you're doing?

Sarah arrived at the station house angry and looking for answers.

"I want to see John!"
"You're going to have to wait Sarah, we are still questioning him."
"About what?"
"Where he got the gun from? Sarah, the gun we found on him is the gun that killed your parents."
"What are you talking about?"
"The gun that John was waving around at me was the same gun that killed your parents. I sent it over to ballistics and the reports says it's a match."
"This isn't happening to me! I should have never trusted him, how could I have been so stupid?"
"Don't blame yourself. You had no way of knowing."

Sarah saw Devon coming through the door and ran into his arms.

"Carl, what's going on?" Said Devon.
"Mr. Williams was waving a gun at me tonight, the same gun that killed Sarah parents'."
"Oh Sarah, I'm sorry."
"No, you're not and I don't blame you. You tried to tell me, but I just wouldn't listen."
"You have a trusting soul, Sarah, and there is nothing wrong with that."
"Oh really. I just let this man into my life without even knowing

anything about him."

"That's just your nature; innocent until proven guilty."

"You know what Devon, you're right; he is innocent until proven guilty. I need to talk to John to hear his side of the story."

"Sarah, haven't you been hurt enough?"

"I've come this far; how can I turn my back on him now?"

"Very easy, they found the murder weapon on him!"

"I need to talk to John. Sheriff Johnson can you take me to him?"

"He is still being processed; it will be a little while longer before anyone can see him."

"What about a lawyer, does he have one?"

"He hasn't asked for one yet."

"I better get on the phone and get him one down here right away."

"Sarah, why don't you wait until you talk to him? Maybe he doesn't want a lawyer."

"It doesn't matter. I'm getting him one."

Sarah couldn't think as she walked the hallways of the Sheriff's Department. She needed to find John a lawyer quick. Not just any lawyer, the best lawyer she could find.

"Devon what are you trying to do to us?"

"What are you talking about, Carl?"

"Innocent until proven guilty! We had her until you said that. She actually believed that he might be guilty. Now she going to hire some hot shot lawyer and this is going to get messy."

"Not if we don't panic, now tell me what happened?"

"I went over there to check out the attic and John came back. I must have left the attic door open. He started up the stairs and I hit him over the head and knocked him out. I left the gun in his hands, went down to the car and called in for back up. I just told them I thought there was an intruder and her house. I went back in stood over the top of him and waited for help to arrive."

"You better make sure you can explain that one!"

"Explain it to whom? I am the Sheriff in this damn town."

"If you think just because you're the Sheriff no one is going to question your story, you're wrong. Remember this is Sarah we are talking about. She won't stop until she thinks she's got the truth."

"She won't be able to prove anything. Especially since she thinks we found the murder weapon on him. He will be out of our hair for good and then it's your turn to take over."

"You act like it's no big deal. Do you really think it was a good idea to plant the gun on him?"

"I thought it was that perfect solution to our problem. She wouldn't be questioning any of this if it wasn't for John. She is going to need you once John is convicted."

"What if she has already found something?"

"She hasn't Devon, or she would be asking questions and she isn't. We have held it together this long we can do it a little longer."

Chapter Thirteen

Sarah had contacted a lawyer from the next town over. She wanted to make sure that whomever she hired had no ties to this community. John deserved the best chance at a fair trial and Sarah was going to make sure that is what he got. The man she hired came with a very good reputation. He had graduated at the top of his class from Harvard.

"Don't worry Ms. Wellington; I'll be there just as soon as I can. Meanwhile, don't let Mr. Williams talk to anyone."
"I won't, but please hurry."

She hung up the phone and felt much better. There was help on the way. She walked back into Sheriff Johnson's office and informed him that she had retained an attorney for John.

"I hope you got the best, he's going to need it."
"Oh don't worry and I have hired the best."
"Who might that be?"
"Mark Phillips."

Sheriff Johnson tried not to show any emotion, but inside he wasn't pleased. He had heard of Mark Phillips and his reputation. They were going to have a battle on their hands.

How could she possible afford Mark Phillips? Along with his reputation, his charges preceded him. Everyone knew that he was very expensive, but was worth every penny.

Sarah could see the fear in his eyes. She was glad now that she had retained him. By the look on Sheriff Johnson face, he wasn't happy with her choice of counsel.

"I hear he's good."

"That's what I understand, now can I please see John, his attorney doesn't want him talking to anyone until he gets here."

"Well then, come this way Sarah and I'll take you to him."

"Do you want me to come along Sarah?" Devon said with fear in his voice.

"No, I want to talk to John alone, Devon."

Sarah walked quickly behind Sheriff Johnson. The only sound she could hear was the clicking of her heels and they hit the floor.

The Sheriff opened the door to the cell where they were holding John. Sarah walked through the cell doors with fear in her eyes.

"Are you okay, John?"

"Who are you?"

"This is no time for jokes John. I need to hear your side of the story."

"I wish I knew what you were talking about lady. Can you tell me who I am and why I'm in jail?"

"He has been talking like this since we arrested him. Claims he doesn't know who he is."

"Can you leave us alone Sheriff? I want to talk to him alone?"

"I don't think that's a good idea Ms. Wellington. He's a dangerous man."

"I'll take my chances, thanks."

"If you say so, just yell when you've had enough. I will leave a deputy outside the door."

Sheriff Johnson turned and locked the cell door behind him. Sarah waited until she heard his foot steps fade down the hallway.

"John, how are you really?"
"I'm fine Sarah."
"You have your memory back?"
"Sarah, be quiet!"
"You never did lose your memory did you?"
"No."
"Why are you trying to make them believe you lost your memory?"
"Because that's what I want them to believe."
"Are you sure were alone?"
"Yes, now tell me what happened?"
"Sarah, I forgot my phone at your house tonight. When I went back to get it, I noticed that the attic door was open and the light was on. I thought for sure that it was Pete Swans. I went up and someone hit me on the back of the head. When I woke up, the sheriff was standing over the top of me and I was in handcuffs. Sarah, the sheriff was in your attic."
"What are you talking about?"
"Sarah, the sheriff planted the gun on me."
"Who planted the gun on you?"
"It must have been the sheriff. He is one who was standing over me when I came to."
"What reason would the sheriff have for planting the gun on you that killed my parents?"
"I don't know Sarah, but you have to believe me."
"I'm trying John, but this just doesn't sound right."
"It is the only explanation for all of this. No one else was there when I came to accept the sheriff. I knew that I had to play it like I had lost his memory. It was the only way I could think of to get us some time to figure this out. Sarah, you have to believe me. I didn't kill your parents."
"What are you saying?"
"The sheriff was in your attic looking for something and I would bet that it has something to do with the papers you found up there."
"I forgot all about the papers, but what would the sheriff want with those."

"I bet this has something to do with your parents' murder?"

"I think I had better get home and get a better look at them."

"Sarah, take them to an attorney as soon as you can. Sarah, this is for real. The proof we have been waiting for just might be in that box of papers. It might even hold the key to who else is behind this."

"I'll be back later John and you be careful."

"You be careful Sarah, if whoever is behind this thinks you have any idea they might come after you."

"I'll be fine John. I'll be back later to see you."

"It doesn't look like I'm going anywhere anytime soon."

"Do you hear something?"

"Yeah, it sounds like someone is coming."

"Hello. You must be Sarah Wellington?"

Sarah looked out the cell door and there stood a very young, very handsome man along side Sheriff Johnson.

"Are you Mark Phillips?"

"In the flesh. You must be John Williams?"

"If you say so."

"Oh, I see he's got a sense of humor."

"Well, not exactly, I think he has amnesia."

"You failed to mention that on the phone."

"I hadn't seen him yet, I had no idea."

"When did this happen?"

"Sometime tonight, he has a lump on the back of this head."

"Sheriff Johnson, can you tell me how he got the lump on his head?"

"I couldn't tell you. He was like this since I found him at Sarah's house waving a gun at me."

"He didn't know who you were when you arrested him?"

"No, he didn't."

"Why when I first came in here did you tell me that I couldn't talk to him because you were questioning him?" Sarah said angrily.

"Because we were questioning him." Sheriff Johnson snapped

back.

"Why didn't you call in a doctor to take a look at him? You knew something was wrong with him?"

"He could be faking."

"Leave us alone, would you please Sheriff Johnson."

"No problem, Mr. Phillips."

"So John, what can you tell me what went on tonight?"

"I can't tell you anything, the last thing I remember is waking up on the floor with the sheriff standing over the top of me."

"Why in this police report does it say that you were waving a gun and him?"

"I don't know!"

"Okay John, I think I need to talk to Sarah alone for a little while. I'll come back and see you later."

"John, are you going to be okay? Do you need anything?"

"I'm fine; just get me out of here."

"We'll be working on that."

Sarah left the cell with Mark not knowing what to think. Could the sheriff have something to do with this or could John be responsible for her parents dying? Maybe this was his way of trying to gain her trust and her sympathy again.

"Ms. Wellington, you realize this is a whole new ball game?"

"You can still help him can't you?"

"Yes, but you have to tell me everything you know."

"I will. Do you want to go somewhere else though?"

"Let's go grab a sandwich. Is there a place that's open?"

"Yes, there is a little diner in town. The foods not great, but it's quiet enough."

"Sounds perfect. I'll follow you there."

"I just want to say good bye to John first."

"Fine, do you want me to come with you?"

"No, I would prefer to go alone."

Sarah walked back to John's cell.

"John, I'm going to talk to the attorney I will have to see you tomorrow."
"You mean I have to stay here?"
"I'm afraid so, I'll be back first thing tomorrow."
"Sarah, I didn't hurt anyone, I promise."
"I know John, I believe you."

Sarah jumped in her car and made sure that Mark was behind her. This is all so bizarre, she thought to herself. I finally thought I was getting somewhere and had someone I truly trusted and was falling in love with. I hope that it wasn't all in vain.

Sarah reached the restaurant and was anxious to talk with Mark. She needed to know if he had a plan and what it was.

She reached the restaurant just as it started to rain. Sarah quickly closed her car door and tried to sprint through the rain drops to the door of the diner. Mark was right behind her as she reached a table and waved the waitress over.

"What can I get you?"
"For starters a hot cup of coffee, would you like something Mr. Phillips?"
"I would love a cup of coffee, please call me Mark though."
"I'm sorry, of course; now where do we begin?"
"You need to tell me everything you know and please start at the beginning."
"It's a really long story."
"That's all right, just tell me what you know."
"Eight years ago my parents were murdered."
"I'm sorry, I didn't know."
"That's okay. I've had time to adjust."
"Please, continue."
"The Sheriff's department didn't have any clues as to what really happened. All they could tell me is that they thought it was a robbery

gone wrong. Then about a week ago John showed up playing a deputy telling me that someone had escaped from prison and wanted to warn me and make sure I was okay. Then I found out he was lying to me and wasn't really a sheriff's deputy."

"How did you find out he way lying?"

"That didn't take much, I just called the local sheriff's department to speak with him and they told me they had never heard of him."

"Didn't you ask to see his badge?"

"No, I wasn't thinking straight; that is my only excuse."

"You could have been hurt."

"I know, but even after I knew he wasn't who he said he was, I still trusted him. Something in his eyes was very soothing."

"Are you sure your trust in him is warranted?"

"I wouldn't have asked for your help if it wasn't."

"Is there more?"

"When I confronted John about his lie, he told me that he was here to protect me. He knew the man who he thought had killed my parents. That same man was in prison until about two weeks ago and then he escaped."

"Who does he think is responsible?"

"The man's name is Pete Swans. I got a phone call from him a couple of nights ago telling me that I should be careful who I let into my house."

"Are you sure it was him?"

"No, but I don't know who else it could have been?"

"Where was John at the time?"

"Out buying a pizza."

"Are you sure he wasn't the one who called you?"

"I'm not sure of anything. Wait, of course I'm sure, it wasn't John."

"How was John's father involved?"

"His father was hired to rob the house, but didn't do the killing."

"Why hasn't he gone to the police?"

"He doesn't have any proof. He was there to rob the house. The man he thinks may have killed my parents he also thinks killed his father."

"Do you know this for a fact?"

"Well not exactly, that's what John told me and I believe him."

"This is a lot to absorb. It doesn't seem possible; I don't know how I'm going to make a jury believe all this?"

"Isn't it called reasonable doubt?"

"You're right, but that's not always as easy as it sounds."

"I never said this would be easy."

"No, I guess you didn't. I'm going to earn my money on this one."

Sarah knew that she couldn't let on that John really hadn't lost his memory. Somehow she had to find a way to find the evidence they needed to prove John was innocent. If John is innocent, then why did the sheriff have the murder weapon and why hadn't he come forward with it.

"I need to get the twenty thousand dollar retainer from you."

"That may be a problem. I'm going to have to sell my house in order to pay you."

"Oh boy, I can feel a pro bono case coming on."

"I'm sorry. I will pay you. It will just take me a little while to get the money together."

"You are taking a really big chance on a man you hardly know."

"I trust him."

"You must. I tell you what, let's just see what happens. If I can win this one, it will earn me the kind of publicity I deserve. Don't worry I do my best work when I don't have much to go on."

"I need to take a look around at your house. Maybe there is something that the police overlooked."

"How about we eat first?"

"I almost forgot about that, let's order."

The food arrived and they sat quietly and ate. Neither one sure what to talk about besides the case and they had already discussed everything Sarah new.

Mark sat wondering how this beautiful woman got mixed up in all this mess. She was young and he could already tell, very hard headed. She was someone to be reckoned with and he wasn't about to tell her that he didn't think John had a chance. It didn't matter how good an attorney he was, they were going to need a miracle to get John off.

They left the restaurant and Sarah lost herself in the drive. Mark was following her home to look for evidence that would help their case. Sarah new that he was holding back something. He may think I'm young, but I can read people very well and if he thinks for one second I don't expect his best, he is sadly mistaken.

They arrived at the house and Sarah ran onto the porch and waited for Mark to join her. She didn't want to touch anything. Sarah wanted to make sure that Mark got the first look around before anything was touched.

"Go ahead, please. I want you to go in first."
"You haven't been inside yet?"
"No and to be perfectly honest with you, I'm not sure I want to."
"What would make you say that?"
"I'm just upset that's all."
"Let's just go in and get this over with. Hopefully the police didn't make a mockery of the crime scene. These small towns have a way of doing that."
"You don't think it's been compromised?"
"Let's hope not."
"I'll wait here while you go in."
"You're really not coming in?"
"Yes, I'm coming. But you go first."
"The police report says that the Sheriff was driving by and noticed suspicious activity in the attic and went to investigate."
"You know that is strange—all in itself. The Sheriff knew that John was helping me and knows what his truck looks like. If John was here, the Sheriff had no reason to investigate."

"What if the sheriff was there first and John surprised him?"

"Is there anything in the attic that John could have been looking for?"

"He's been helping me clean it out. The roof was really bad and a lot needed to be thrown out up there. So yes, it's possible that John had a reason to be in the attic."

Sarah knew she wasn't telling the truth. John wasn't supposed to be in the attic when she wasn't with him. They had agreed that they would go through the boxes together. She wasn't about to tell Mark that though.

"Sarah, do you believe he lost his memory?"

"What reason would he have for faking?"

"You tell me. You know him."

"No, I don't believe he is faking. It scares me though; he was my only link to what really happened to my parents."

"Maybe it's guilt that's blocking out his memory?"

"He doesn't have anything to feel guilty about. He was trying to protect me."

"Are you sure this Pete Swans even exists?"

"He has to; John wouldn't have made that up."

"Do you ever remember your mother or father talking about Swans?"

"No, I had never heard the name before."

"We have to be missing something. What could he have been after?"

"That's the confusing part. My parents didn't have a lot of money. Their life insurance policies were just enough to pay for my college education."

"What did your mother and father do for a living?"

"My dad sold insurance and my mother was a house wife."

"What kind of insurance did you dad sell?"

"All kinds I guess, I wasn't really interested in his career. I was only eighteen when he died."

"He must have sold life insurance too then."

"I suppose, why do you ask?"

"How much money did you receive when they were killed?"

"Fifty thousand dollars."

"I can't believe that you dad sold life insurance and only had a twenty-five thousand-dollar policy on himself and your mother; especially since they had you?"

"He probably didn't think he was going to die."

"No one thinks they are going to die. This just doesn't make any sense. We are definitely missing a piece of the puzzle."

"I don't understand what you are talking about. Why does it matter how much life insurance my parents had?"

"Maybe it doesn't, but I think it is something we definitely need to look into. Now where is the attic?"

"Right through the kitchen."

"I think I'll take a look around up there. Are you coming?"

"If it's alright with you, I think I would rather stay here."

"That's fine; I'll be back in a minute."

Sarah sat at the kitchen table waiting for Mark to emerge from the attic. Hoping he would find something that would prove John didn't do what the Sheriff said he had done.

Mark came through the attic door and Sarah jumped to her feet.

"Well, did you find anything?"

"I'm sorry Sarah, I didn't."

"What do we do now?"

"I am going to do some snooping around tomorrow. If you need to get a hold of me you can reach me on my cell phone."

"What's got you so worried? I can tell something is wrong by the look on your face."

"Something just isn't adding up?"

"Are you going to tell me what's going on?"

"I'm not sure if anything, but I will call you tomorrow. You get some rest and let me worry about it."

Mark left Sarah very uneasy. Between her parents being murdered here and now with what happened to John she was more than ready to put this house in her past. Even if that meant having no place to live.

Sarah wasn't ready to sleep, but she went to bed any way.

She laid there thinking about John and how much she missed him. Her life would never be the same if she didn't get him back. It didn't feel the same in the house without John there.

Sarah awoke and quickly looked at the alarm clock on her night stand. It was only two thirty in the morning. She heard a noise coming from the living room. Great, someone is in the house and no one was is here to protect me.

Her mind began to whirl with fear. Sarah, have you lost your mind. You haven't ever needed anyone to protect you before.

Think, what do you do? She quietly raised herself from the bed and looked for her cell phone. She was going to call the police first and then get up and take a look around.

She bent down over her purse as someone grabbed her from behind. Sarah could feel terror come over her like a tidal wave. She was spun around before she could even react.

John was standing there and kissed her as he watched the fear leave her eyes.

"John, what are you doing here? How did you get out of jail?"

"They let me go because the evidence they had wasn't enough to hold me any longer."

"I want to make love to you Sarah. I couldn't take it if some how they convicted me and I had to sit in prison for the rest of my life never knowing how it felt to make love to you."

"I understand John and I would feel the same way. I'm not quite sure I know that this is the best thing for us, but I couldn't stand the thought of it either."

John grabbed her and kissed her for the first time with raw passion. Sarah moaned softly and returned his kiss with as much passion. He picked her up and threw her on the bed under him. He slowly started kissing her neck and found his way to her nipples. It had been a long time since Sarah had been intimate with anyone and John's touch was almost more than she could handle. She lay motionless as he kissed every inch of her body. The urge was too great for her to take anymore. She reached out for him. She wanted to feel him inside her. A feeling of pure joy came over her as she felt him enter. They melted together like one wave in one ocean. She couldn't keep silent as she moaned with all she had in her. Sarah didn't want it to end. She wanted him to stay there forever. She felt complete and she drifted back to sleep wrapped in his arms.

Sarah was awoken by the beeping of her alarm clock. She rolled over to shut off the alarm clock and realized that John wasn't in bed.

"John, where are you?"

She got of bed and walked around the house yelling his name. A knock on the front door startled her.

"John?"

She flung open the door with great excitement, only to find Devon standing there.

"Did I hear you yelling John?"
"Yes, he was here last night and this morning he was gone."
"Sarah, John is still in jail."
"No, he said they released him because they didn't have enough evidence to hold him."
"Sarah, please believe me. I just left him in his cell."
"You mean it was all a dream?"
"From the look on your face, I'm guessing it was an interesting one. So tell me, what do you know about Mark Phillips?"
"I just know he is the best we've got around here."
"How are you going to pay him?"
"I will sell the house if I have to."

"Sarah, have you lost your mind?"

"It feels like it this morning."

"I won't let you sell this house to pay for John's defense."

"You really don't have a say in the matter Devon."

"Be reasonable, where will you live?"

"Oh don't panic Devon; Mark is willing to defend John without my money for now."

"Why would he do that?"

"I don't know Devon and I really don't care as long as he defends him."

"Aren't you the least bit curious why this man would want to help you? I swear Sarah sometimes you are so naive."

"What are you talking about?"

"You're a beautiful young woman, Sarah. Can't you see that?"

"You are the one jumping to conclusions, Devon. Can't someone just be willing to help without wanting to jump into bed with me?"

"Oh, what, like John?"

"We are not talking about John now Devon. I think you have some issues that you need to deal with and quit worrying about me."

"I can't help it Sarah. I feel obligated to look out for you."

"Well don't. I can take care of myself!"

"Sarah, I didn't come over here to fight with you, I just wanted to make sure you were okay. I'm sorry if I said something I shouldn't have."

"Let's just forget it."

"Are you going to talk to John this morning?"

"As soon as I pull myself together."

"Do you want me to wait and give you a lift?"

"Thanks, but I think I'd rather drive myself. I will talk to you at the office when I'm done."

"Will I see you later?"

"I'll be in as soon as I see John."

"Don't take too long, I have some files I need you to go through."

"Oh Devon, why do you have to pull that on me this morning?"

"You still have a job to do!"

"I know Devon. I haven't forgotten."
"What time do you think you might make it in?"
"I will be in as soon as I finish talking to John."
"Okay, Okay, take your time."
"I'll see you later."

Chapter Fourteen

Sarah arrived at the prison as John was finishing breakfast. She was so glad to see him except for the look of fear in his eyes.

"Good morning John, how are you today?"
"As good as can be expected in here."
"I'm sorry John; I'm doing everything I can to get you out of here."
"Why are you so willing to help me?"
"Because I love you John!"
"After every thing that has happened?"
"Yes, I love you."

Sarah couldn't believe the words that just come out of her mouth. She was amazed and relieved all at the same time. It felt good to be able to say that to him.

"I love you too Sarah. So what's the plan?"
"I'm not sure, John. I need to get to work though."
"You need to take the papers into the attorney to look at them."
"I will on my way to the office."
"Will you come back and see me later?"
"Of course I will, as soon as I get out of work."

Sarah jumped in her car and raced home. What could possibly be in those papers that my parents had to die for? She flung open the front door and raced into the bedroom where she had hidden the papers. She opened the box and began reading them one by one. The first was the deed to her house which she had originally thought. As she got deeper into the box, she found a lot of death certificates and life insurance policies for people she had never heard of. What was her father doing with all of these? Who are all these people?

I think I need to find out who some of these people are. She picked up the box and headed for the front door. The library has to keep records of deaths in this town.

She grabbed five death certificates and put the rest of the box in her trunk. Sarah raced to the library and immediately starting questioning the librarian.

"Where can I find information on deaths from five to ten years ago?"
"They are all on micro film by date?"
"Can you show me where?"
"Certainly, follow me."

Sarah found a quiet spot in the corner and picked up the first death certificate. Robert Thompson, date of death January 15, 1991. It took her a little while to find an article on his death. It seems his car flipped over on a less-traveled road. A snow storm hit and his car was covered in snow. He wasn't found until four days later. He was only thirty one the day he died and there were no known survivors.

Sarah found his life insurance policy which was worth one hundred thousand dollars. It was collected on August 21st, 1991 by Jonathan Peterson.

If this man had no living relatives than who is this Jonathan Peterson and why did he collect the life insurance money? This is getting stranger all the time, Sarah thought to herself. She moved onto the next one and slowly read through the life insurance policy. The date of death was March 2, 1995. Again the person had no living relatives and the money was again collected by Jonathan Peterson.

As she went through the other three, she found the same thing on each, no living relatives and the money was collected by Jonathan Peterson.

I need to find out who Jonathan Peterson is and what connection he would have to these five people.

Sarah went back to the librarian to help her find a listing of birth records.

"Can you tell me where I can find a listing of birth records please?"
"Certainly, what are you researching?"
"Oh, just trying to research my family tree."
"Very interesting, the birth records are in this section over here. Again they are kept by date."
"Thanks so much. You have been a huge help."

Sarah waited for her to walk back to the front desk before she began rummaging through the dates. Let see, it says here that Jonathan Peterson was born on March 23, 1955. Sarah found the register for 1955 and began searching for the name Jonathan Peterson. There was no record of his birth which meant he wasn't born in this town. I suppose it couldn't have been that easy.

Sarah quickly picked up the information she had gathered and returned to the prison to see John.

Chapter Fifteen

"Well, what did the attorney have to say about the papers?"
"I haven't taken them in yet."
"Why not?"
"I wanted to do some investigating on my own."
"Sarah, this is dangerous stuff. You need to take that into Mark Phillips."
"I will John, I promise. I just have a couple of more things I want to look into."
"Sarah, please don't mess around with this. If something happens to you, I will never forgive myself."
"I promise John. I will take them to him this afternoon."
"I found out something interesting."
"What?"
"When I started going through the box, I found some insurance claims that all had the same name listed as beneficiary."
"Who is listed as the beneficiary?"
"Jonathon Peterson, does that name sound familiar you?"
"No, not at all. Please Sarah, turn over the papers to Mark. You are going to need help with this and with me stuck in here; I don't want you doing this alone. Maybe the answers lie in that box?"
"I don't understand how this could have anything to do with my parents' murder."
"I don't either Sarah, but please go show Mark the papers."
"I will."
"Now!"

"Hey, don't yell at me!"

"I don't mean to, I just want this over with. I'm sorry."

"It's okay and I'm sorry too. It's almost like I'm afraid to find the answers now."

"Sarah, we have to find the answer; otherwise, we will never be together."

"Why are you saying that?"

"Sarah, I'm in prison and they planted the murder weapon on me. They are going to nail me for your parents' murder."

"Are you sure you didn't have it the whole time?"

"What are you saying?"

"Nothing John, I just thought maybe your dad had the gun on him when he came home and you didn't realize that it was the murder weapon."

"Sarah, my dad didn't own a gun and he didn't come home with one."

"I'm sorry."

"Don't you believe that he planted it on me Sarah?"

"I guess so. What is happening John?"

"I don't know Sarah; I just know something isn't adding up."

"I need to find some answers. Will you be all right?"

"I'll be fine. Please be careful."

"Oh don't worry, I will. I don't trust anyone right now."

"Make sure you go right to the attorney, okay. Don't tell anyone what you have found."

"I won't. I'll be back later."

Sarah drove straight to Mark Phillips office. She didn't realize that a Sheriff Johnson had followed her from the prison.

Sheriff Johnson sat is his car making sure to keep his distance. What is that girl up to? I think it is time to take her out of the picture no matter what Devon says. He watched patiently as she removed the box from her trunk. I have to get to her before she brings that box into the attorneys office. He jumped out of the car and ran toward Sarah.

"Sarah, what are you doing?"

"Hello Sheriff, nice day isn't it?"

"Sarah, I asked you a question. What are you doing?"

"I'm here discussing John's case with the attorney I hired."

"What's in the box?"

"Just some legal papers of my parents. I thought as long as I have him on a retainer, I would get him to take a look at them."

"You're not withholding any evidence that pertains to Mr. Williams are you?"

"No, I'm not."

"Sarah, I want you to give me the box."

"Oh, I don't think so. It's just some papers of my parents."

"If that is true Sarah, I will return them to you, but for right now I want the papers."

"Hello Ms. Wellington, how are you today?"

"I was fine until I ran into the Sheriff here."

"What seems to be the problem?"

"I found this box of papers at my parents' house and I wanted you take a look at them. The Sheriff thinks that they have something to do with John's case and wants me to turn them over to him."

"Is that true Sheriff?"

"I just recommended that she turn them over."

"Well, that's good to hear. Of course I will take a look at them. Sheriff, if I find anything of interest to you, I'll be sure to let you know."

Sheriff Johnson left and went back to his car. I hope she was telling me the truth and all that was in that box were papers of her parents. If that girl has figured any of this out that changes everything. I need to call Devon. He has to call Sarah and find out how much she knows.

"Devon, it's Carl. I followed Sarah today. She pulled out a box out of her trunk that she was delivering to her attorney. The box looked just like the other boxes in her attic."

"So what? It was a box."

"Did you ever think that it might have some incriminating evidence in it?"

"Carl you need to calm down."

"Calm down, how can you tell me to calm down?"

"We don't know what's in the box. If you panic you'll be nailing our coffin shut."

"What are we supposed to do now?"

"Nothing, just be patient. I will call Sarah later and see what I can find out."

"Aren't you the least bit nervous?"

"Carl, even if she has what you think she has, there is nothing to link us to it."

"You're the one who told me that she wouldn't stop until she got all the answers."

"Yes, I know, but if we over react we will only help her out."

"You're joking right? What are we supposed to do? Just sit back and let her bury us?"

"Carl, just take a deep breath and worry about getting John convicted. I will handle Sarah."

"You had better be Devon."

Devon sat back in his chair and let out a big sigh. *I have to think, because obviously Carl isn't. What could she have in that box? I can't believe that it's anything to worry about. At least I don't think so.*

Chapter Sixteen

"I was so glad to see you."
"What's going on Sarah?"
"I found this box in the attic and I think you need to take a look at it."
"What is it?"
"You tell me, that's why I am here."
"Well let's go inside and take a look."

Mark sat for a long time in silence looking through the papers.

"Sarah, do you know what you have here?"
"I think so; they are life insurance policies of people who were all collected by the same person."
"We need to find out who this Jonathan Peterson is."
"I can tell you that he wasn't born around here. I checked for his birth records at the library."
"Did you ever think that it could be an alias?"
"Do you think it could be?"
"I don't know, but I think we should consider it."
"What do we do now?"
"You do nothing. If whoever is behind this finds out what you have found, you could be in a lot of danger."
"Oh please, another man who thinks I can't take care of myself."
"Quit acting like that."
"Quit treating me like I'm a helpless woman."

"Oh, you are going to drive me crazy. I am serious. You could be in a lot of danger."

"Yeah, I know. What do you suggest I do?"

"Just, sit back and let me go to work."

"You mean I can't help you."

"No Sarah, you need to pretend that what you brought me were just some legal papers of your parents. We don't want to make anyone suspicious."

"Will you call me later if you find out anything?"

"Oh course. Now please go to work, go home or do whatever it is you would normally being doing."

"I will. Please call me at the office if you find anything."

"I will, but don't talk to anyone."

Sarah left Mark's office in a daze. How could any of this be happening? Why did John have to bring all this on me? I was happy before in my own little world and now I feel like it's all falling apart.

She returned to the prison and ran right into the Sheriff.

"Well hello again, did you have a nice visit with your attorney?"

"Yes, as a matter of fact. I found out some interesting things about my parents."

"Well that's great, as long as you're not withholding evidence."

"I would never do that Sheriff."

"Can I see John now, please?"

"Yes, no problem. You know his preliminary hearing his set for next week?"

"Yes, but thanks for telling me."

"I hope your attorney is spending time on his case, because he is going to need it."

"Thanks for your concern, but I think he'll be fine. After all he has the best attorney around. Now I'm going to see John, would you please let me in?"

"Wilkes, let Ms. Wellington into cell #12."

"Thank you."

Sarah walked down the long hallway to John's cell and knew that Sheriff Johnson was watching her very closely. She had to remember what Mark told her. No one can suspect anything. She had to be as nonchalant as possible.

"John, how are you?"
"What did Mark have to say about the papers?"
"That something is going on. Were just not sure what yet."
"Are the papers what you thought they were?"
"Yes, but we don't know what it means. He's going to do some checking today. I think we need to talk about something else. There are too many ears around."
"You're right, can I have a kiss?"
"You are supposed to have lost your memory; do you think that's a good idea?"
"I guess not, but I miss you so much. I wish I hadn't been so stupid. If I hadn't forgotten my phone at your house, I wouldn't be in this situation."
"John it's all going to work out, I promise."
"I have to get to work now, I will try to come back later and see you."
"I love you Sarah."
"I love you too, John. I'll see you later."

Sarah arrived at work fifteen minutes later and Devon was sitting at her desk.

"Hey, what are you doing in here?"
"Waiting for you."
"Is something wrong?"
"I got a call from Sheriff Johnson this afternoon."
"Oh, what did he want?"
"Sarah, don't play dumb with me. Are you withholding evidence?"
"The sheriff is crazy and who are you to question me?"
"I'm your friend and I'm trying to make sure that you don't land

yourself in jail for obstruction of justice."

"Devon, that's not going to happen."

"I wouldn't be so sure. What did you bring to the attorney if it wasn't evidence?"

"Like I told the sheriff, it was just some papers of my parents that I didn't understand. I just want him to look over them."

"I could have looked at them for you."

"That's okay, but it's no big deal—really."

"Are you sure?"

"Oh I'm sure, now would you please let me get to work."

"Maybe you should take a break from all this for a little while. Get out of town, go on vacation."

"I can't leave right now and John needs me."

"You will do John a lot more good if you get some rest."

Sarah's phone began to ring and she was glad. It gave her an excuse to get Devon out of her office and her hair.

"Hello, Sarah Wellington speaking, may I help you."

"Sarah, it's Mark Phillips."

"Oh hello, can you hold on a minute?"

"Of course."

"Devon, I need to take this. Would you mind if we finish this conversation later?"

"Okay, if you promise me you will consider what I said?"

"Okay."

Devon walked out of Sarah's office and made sure that he didn't quite shut the door. He had to know what she was up to.

"Thanks for holding, did you find out anything?"

"I have a friend who is a private investigator. I have him out looking for this Jonathon Peterson."

"How long will that take?"

"Just a couple of days I hope."

"We don't have a couple of days."

"Sarah, you need to let me do my job."

"I know, it's just my whole life seems like it's turned up side down."

"I know Sarah, but I think we are on to something. In the box you brought me there were ten insurance policies with all the same beneficiaries."

"Jonathan Peterson is the beneficiary on all the policies?"

"You got it and whoever he is he's a very rich man. The policies total about five million dollars."

"I still don't understand what this has to do with my parents."

"My guess is that your father found about this Jonathan Peterson or whoever he is and was on the verge of busting it wide open."

"That's means that John was right and Swans was working for someone."

"It looks like it."

"You don't know how much better that makes me feel."

"I will call you as soon as I find out anything."

"Thanks Mark, I appreciate your help."

"Good-Bye."

Well, so she does know more than she letting on. I have to get a hold of Carl and fill him in. Devon walked away from Sarah's door trying not to make a noise. He went back to his office and shut the door behind him.

"Hello, Sheriffs Department, may I help you."

"Give me Sheriff Johnson please."

"May I tell him who is calling?"

"It's Devon Grant, you idiot."

"Oh, I'm sorry Mr. Grant, I'll put you right through."

"Sheriff Johnson speaking, how can I help you?"

"We have a big problem."

"Is that you Devon?"

"Yes, it's me. Did you hear what I said?"

"I thought we didn't have anything to worry about. Isn't that what you said?"

"She has found the insurance policies and she knows that the beneficiary on them is Jonathon Peterson."

"You don't think they will connect that to us?"

"I hope not, or we will never get out of this."

"What do you want me to do?"

"I don't know Carl. I think we've taken this too far already."

"No kidding, but we need to take care of this."

"What are you suggesting?"

"Don't play with me."

"You seem to have forgotten, I have as much at stake here as you. The only reason I agreed to help you with this at all is we are best friends. I don't plan on going to prison for you though."

"It won't let it get that far. I'll talk to you later."

Devon hung up the phone and sat back in his chair in disbelief. How could this be happening? I love that girl and I wish there was something I could do. I wish she had never met John and none of this would have happened. Now he will have to live with his decision.

"Knock, Knock."

"Come in."

"Devon, I just wanted to stop by before I went home to tell you I'm sorry."

"Come in and sit down."

"I'm tired Devon and I just want to go home."

"Do you want to grab some dinner?"

"No, I haven't had much of an appetite lately."

"You still should try to eat something."

"I'll be fine and I'll see you in the morning."

"Sarah, be careful."

"Why do you keep saying that?"

"I am just worried about you. You need to take care of yourself."

"I always take care of myself; I'm used to it by now."

"You haven't made many good decisions lately."

"What do you mean by that?"

"Are you telling me that you think John was a good decision?"

"I think it was. He makes me feel alive."

"Sarah, he is in prison for killing your parents."

"He is accused of killing my parents and he hasn't been convicted yet. I thought you of all people would understand."

"Understand what?"

"That just because all the evidence points in one direction doesn't mean that is where the truth lies. You taught me that when I came to work for you. You always told me to trust my heart when the truth was hard to see."

"I know, but I also told you that sometimes the evidence is overwhelming and then you have to do what is right."

"I am doing what is right. I defending the man I love."

"Oh Sarah, I can't believe you just said that. How can you love a man you have only known for a little over a week?"

"I don't know. I just know I do. I feel very safe when I'm with John and I don't know what I would do without him."

"You may find out if he is convicted."

"I don't think that is going to happen."

"You don't know what the future holds and I hate to see you get hurt. I told your father that I would watch out for you and I'm apparently not doing a very good job."

"When did you tell my father that?"

"The night he died."

"You never told me that you saw him the night he died."

"I know I didn't. I knew you would have questions and I wasn't up to telling you the details."

"I have so many questions for you. Did my mother suffer? Did my father suffer? Oh my God, did they tell who was responsible?"

"No Sarah, I don't know who was responsible. Don't you think if I knew, they wouldn't be in prison already?"

"I would hope so."

"Did they suffer Devon?"

"No Sarah, they didn't suffer. That I can tell you for sure."

"Every time I turn around, I feel like I am reliving that night all over again."

"I'm sorry, I made a promise to your father and I intend on keeping it."

"I was a child then and I'm not anymore. You don't have to protect me anymore."

"It's not that easy. Did you think any more about going on vacation?"

"Yes, but no. I can't leave right now. Maybe when this is all over."

"It may be too late then Sarah."

"Too late?"

"Oh never mind. Go home and get some rest."

"Devon, what did you mean by that?"

"Nothing really, just go home and get some rest."

"I'll see you tomorrow, maybe then you can explain to me what you're talking about."

"Good night Sarah."

"Good night Devon."

Sarah's ride home was long and lonely. I miss John so much, she thought to herself. My life wouldn't be the same without him. What am I going to do if he is convicted? Her thoughts were interrupted by the ringing of her phone.

"Hello."

"Hello Sarah, it's Mark Phillips."

"Did you find anything out?"

"Where are you?"

"Driving in my car, why?"

"Would you mind coming over to my office?"

"Did you find something?"

"I need to talk to you; can you please just come over to my office?"

"I'll be there in ten minutes."

He has got me nervous now. This may be the moment of truth

and I'm not sure if I'm ready to handle it. I guess there is no turning back now.

Sarah rushed over to Mark's office. He was waiting outside when she arrived.

"What's going on?"
"Come in and we'll talk about it."
"Mark, you need to tell me what's going on!"
"I will, just get in here."
"Okay, I'm in, now what is going on."
"I think I've figured out who Jonathan Peterson is?"
"Oh my God, who is it?"
"You may want to sit down."
"Mark, for heavens sakes, just tell me."
"I believe it is Devon Grant."
"No, it can't be."
"My PI is quite sure it is."
"How?"
"Their social security numbers match."
"This is some kind of joke, right?"
"I wish it was. The files you found may only be the tip of the iceberg. I've already shown Sheriff Johnson the evidence and told him that I want Devon arrested. He is on his way over there right now."
"I can't believe this is happening. It can't be true."
"I have to find the proof that Devon had your parents killed. Your dad must have figured out what Devon was up to and was going to turn him in."
"Did you say that you showed Sheriff Johnson the evidence?"
"That's correct, why?"
"Mark, we have a real problem now."
"What now?"
"John thinks that the Sheriff planted the gun on him."
"What reason would the sheriff have for doing that?"
"He has to be involved some how in all of this. If the sheriff is on

his way over there, he could be warning Devon to get out of town."

"I had better get over there."

"What about me?"

"You go home and wait for my call."

"I can't do that. There is too much at stake here for me."

"I'm not arguing with you right now Sarah, go home!"

"You had better call me later."

"I will, hey by the way when did he tell you that he thought the sheriff had planted the gun on him?"

"This morning when I went to talk to him."

"I thought he lost his memory. How did he remember that?"

"That is another story all by itself."

"Well, you had better clue me in."

"Maybe when this is over."

"No, I think you should tell me now."

"Okay, Okay, he was faking it."

"Why didn't you tell me?"

"I didn't want to tell you something that would jeopardize John's defense. That doesn't matter now though."

"We still have to find the proof to link this all together, and if John thinks the Sheriff is involved, that's going to make this a whole lot more difficult."

"I know you can put this together."

"I hope so Sarah, it won't look good if they find out John was faking."

"We just won't tell them."

"That's fine for now, but eventually we will have to."

"Why?"

"We have to have a reason to investigate the sheriff. Without John's testimony, we will have nothing to corroborate all the evidence."

"Are you sure they will believe him?"

"That's why we have juries."

"What if we can find the proof to link him to this on our own?"

"Then we won't need John."

"Maybe Devon will roll on the sheriff himself."

"Oh, you don't know Devon like I do. He will deny this all the way."

"It won't matter if we find the proof. Especially if we can trace the money back to him."

"I wish this wasn't true. It seems impossible when I think about it. Devon has always looked out for me. Only to find out that he could be responsible for all the pain. I'm not sure I will ever forgive him."

"That would be understandable."

"What do we do next?"

"You need to go home and get some rest. You have been through so much."

"I'm fine, really. Just let me help."

"Sarah, that isn't a good idea and you know it."

"What am I supposed to do? The man I love is in jail and a man I've known and trusted for the better part of my life is on his way to jail."

"I need to go and I will call you when I know something."

Mark left in a hurry and Sarah found herself alone again. Her whole life was falling apart around her. It all seemed so unreal.

Chapter Seventeen

Sheriff Johnson arrived at Devon office and walked through the front door and right into his office.

"What brings you down here?"
"I just left Mark Phillips office. He has about of ten life insurance policies in his possession that show Jonathan Peterson as the beneficiary. He matched your social security number to them and wants you arrested."
"I have to get out of here then."
"Oh no, you're not leaving me holding the bag."
"What do you suggest I do then, just let you arrest me?"
"You don't have a choice right now. If I don't arrest you and let you walk out of here not only will they will think you are guilty, but that I also am some how involved."
"You are involved and you're just trying to cover your own ass."
"I am not. I'm trying to cover both of our asses."
"What if they find out the rest and put two and two together? I'm not going to prison Carl!"
"No, you're not. Just let me handle this."

Mark jumped in his car and headed over to Devon's office. He wasn't sure what he would find when he got there. He pulled up and the Sheriff's car was parked outside the entrance. He opened the front door to the building. Ms. Lewis, Devon's secretary was sitting at her desk with a look of confusion on her face.

"I need to see the Sheriff and Mr. Grant please. Tell them Mr. Phillips is here to see them."

"Mr. Grant, Mr. Phillips is here to see you."

The door to the office was flung open in a rage.

"What do you want?"

"Just checking to make sure that the sheriff is doing his job."

"You are crazy, do you know that? I don't know what kind of evidence you think you have, but I haven't done anything wrong."

"Can you tell me who Jonathan Peterson is?"

"How am I supposed to know?"

"Your social security number matches his?"

"So some guy stole my social security number."

"Why did you pay him more than five million dollars in life insurance policies if he was using your social security number?"

"You think you have the truth, but you don't."

"Well then, please enlighten me."

"You don't understand. It's not that simple."

"Well then, I guess you're going to prison."

"I didn't want it to come to this."

"You mean you didn't want to get caught?"

"It was Sarah's father who was on the take. I got suspicious when I started doing an annual audit. That's when I found out something was wrong. I never looked very closely at his work. I trusted him. He would bring me in claims and I would sign off on them. I never even looked to see who the beneficiary was. When I arrived at the house that night with the Sheriff, Sarah's mother was dead and her father was fading fast. He said he was sorry and that we needed to protect Sarah. Pete Swans had tried to get more money out of him. When he wouldn't give in he said he would kill Sarah. He told him that he would never get paid and then shot himself. John's father tried to reason with Swans, but he wouldn't listen. Swan's shot John's father.

Swans must have heard us pull up and booked it out of there. John's father managed to get up and walk out. We heard later that he had died from the gunshot wound."

"Why didn't you turn him in? Why does Sarah think it was a robbery then?"

"Because that's what we told her. I couldn't tell her the truth. It would have crushed her. Her old man was a prince in her eyes."

"That doesn't explain why the sheriff planted the murder weapon on Mr. Williams?"

"What are you talking about?"

"Sheriff, John remembers everything, including you planting the gun on him."

"That's my fault."

"Oh, I would like to see you to explain that one to me."

"I knew Sarah was getting close to figuring this all out and I couldn't stand to see her get hurt. John was an easy choice to frame for her parents murder. It would get him out of her life. I didn't want her finding out the truth and besides I was in love with her. With him in the picture I didn't have a chance."

"If you knew all this, why didn't you have Swans arrested?"

"He was under arrest and in prison until about two weeks ago."

"For something else though. There was never any mention of what you're telling me."

"That's because I couldn't let anyone find out about this. I couldn't take the chance that Sarah would find out the truth."

"You don't think Swans would come after Sarah do you? Looking for her to pay her father's debt?"

"He wouldn't be that stupid."

"Sheriff, you need to go release John and hope he doesn't press charges against both of you. I'm going to check on Sarah, we need to find Swans and get him back in prison where he belongs. You two better hope this whole thing doesn't blow up in your faces."

"I know we were wrong, but we were just thinking of Sarah."

"Well, you obviously weren't thinking very clearly at all."

Mark hopped in the car and headed over to Sarah's house.

Chapter Eighteen

Sarah got home and couldn't even think straight. I can't believe that Devon could be behind all this. It seems impossible to believe. I know things will be better tomorrow. They should have to release John soon. Just thinking of him makes me feel better.

She dropped her keys on the coffee table and headed for the bedroom. A hot shower should make me feel better and then a good night sleep.

Sarah gathered up her pajamas and headed for the bathroom. The hot water felt wonderful and actually made her feel a little sleepy. Maybe I will be able to sleep tonight after all.

Sarah bent over and grabbed the nozzle to turn off the water when she was ripped from the shower and slammed on her back. The pain shot through her like a bullet. What was happening. Her head was spinning with pain. She began to feel the back of her head getting very warm from the blood that was running out from the back of her head onto to the floor around her. She was suddenly being pulled up by her hair as it was being ripped from her head.

"I want my money?"
"Who are you? What do you want?"
"I want my money."
"I don't know what you are talking about."
"Don't play stupid with me. Where did your father hide the money?"

"I don't know what you're talking about."
"Fine then I guess I'll just have to kill you."

Sarah suddenly began to cry with fear. Her whole body ached with pain. Sarah, think, you need to keep your head on straight. Oh my God, it's got to be Pete Swans. Why is he asking where my father hid the money? Play along Sarah. You have to survive for John.

"Okay, I'll tell you where the money is."
"That's more like it, now where is it?"
"Can I get some clothes on?"
"Just tell me where the money is?"
"I'll get it for you just let me get some clothes on."
"Hurry up and don't think you can play me, or I will have to hurt you."
"All right, just let me dry off and get my clothes on."

Sarah grabbed a towel and headed for the bedroom.

"Where do you think you're going?"
"To get my clothes."
"Just put those on."
"I'm not going to change in front of you."

Sarah closed the door only to have Pete Swans push it open in a mad thrust.

"Do I look stupid to you or something?"
"I'm not going to get dressed with you watching me."
"Oh, I'm afraid you are."
"Could you at least turn around?"
"Listen, I'm not fooling around. I want you to take me to the money right now or I will kill you."
"Fine."

Sarah you have to think. Why didn't you buy a damn gun? I will just get dressed and find an opportunity to get away from him.

"Let's go, I don't have all night."

Swans grabbed the back of her neck for pure enjoyment.

"It's a shame I don't have more time. I would enjoy you."

Sarah cringed at the thought and suddenly became a lot clearer about her situation.

"Would you please let me go so I can get you the money?"
"Okay, but I'm watching you."

They walked through the kitchen to the attic door.

"Don't try to get away from me or I'm going to have to hurt you."
"You will never find the money then, now will you."
"Don't play with me little girl. I will hurt you so bad."

Chapter Nineteen

Mark knew he needed to get to Sarah. She had to know the truth and it seemed he was going to be the only one who would tell her.

Sheriff Johnson opened the door to John's cell and sat down beside him.

"What do you want?"
"I'm here to tell you the truth."
"What do you know about the truth?"
"John, Sarah's father was behind all of this. Devon and I were just trying to protect her."
"What are you talking about?"
"I know you never lost your memory so you can stop pretending."
"What did you mean; Sarah's father was behind all this?"
"He had an insurance scam going. He listed Jonathan Peterson as the beneficiary on a lot of insurance policies. Devon didn't figure it out until it was too late. He went to confront him and he walked in as he was about to pull the trigger. He tried to talk him out of it, but it was no use. He told him about Pete Swans and your father. Sarah's father hired Pete Swans and your father to steal the insurance policies. That way there would be no physical evidence to link him to the money. He used Devon's social security number so that if anyone got suspicious they would blame Devon. He told Devon that Pete Swans had gotten greedy and didn't want to share the money with your father so he shot him. He couldn't live with the guilt any more,

so he killed himself."
"Does Sarah know about this?"
"Mr. Phillips is on his way over there right now to tell her."
"You need to take me to her. She is going to need me now."

Mark pulled up to Sarah house and ran up to the front door. He began knocking frantically and calling her name.

"Sarah, open the door it's Mark Phillips."

When Sarah didn't come to the door Mark got worried. Something isn't right here. I need to get talk to the sheriff. He slowly stepped off the porch and got back in his car.

"Sheriffs' department, how can I help you?"
"I need to talk to Sheriff Johnson and it's an emergency."
"One minute please."
"Sheriff Johnson speaking."
"I'm at Sarah's house and she isn't answering the door."
"Who is this?"
"It's Mark Phillips."
"Maybe she is sleeping."
"I don't think so. All her lights are on."
"Where are you?"
"I'm in my car outside her house."
"Stay there, I'll be right over."

Mark hung up the phone and tried to think. I have to get in there and help her. He could kill her by the time the sheriff gets here.

"What's going on?"
"Mr. Phillips is at Sarah's house and she isn't answering the door."
"You don't think Swans has her do you?"
"Calm down John. I'll go over there and check it out."
"If something happens to her I will kill you. Let's go we have to

help her."
"You're not going anywhere."
"Oh, try to stop me. I love her and no one is going to hurt her."
"All right you can go, but you stay in the car."
"Whatever, lets just get out of here."

"You better not be taking me on a wild goose chase. I wasn't kidding when I said I would kill you."
"I don't doubt it. The money is right up here."
"Hurry up, get up the stairs."

Sarah walked slowly up stairs trying to stay calm and think with every step she took.

"Okay, now where is the money?"
"How do I know you're not going to kill me when I tell you where the money is?"
"You don't have a choice; I will kill you if you don't tell me where it is."
"It's buried over there behind those boards."
"Well get over there and show me where."
"I'm telling you, that's where it is?"

Swans grabbed her by the nape of the neck and pushed her.
"Stand here and don't move do you understand me?"
"Yes."

Swans started to pound at the boards with his fists. The sound was ringing through Sarah ears like a piercing lightening bolt.
Outside Sheriff Johnson pulled up next to Mark's car. Mark jumped out and ran towards John.
"We have to get in there John, I think Swans has her."
"I think so to. What are we going to do?"
"You two are going to stay here while I have a look around."
"I love her and no one is going to keep me away from her."

"John, do you want her alive?"
"That's a stupid question, of course I do."
"Then stay out here and let me do my job."
"Bring her back to me sheriff, please."
"I will John."

Mark and John waited outside as the sheriff made his way around to the back of the house.

"If I lose her now Mr. Phillips I don't know what I would do."
"You can't talk like John. I'm sure Sarah will be fine."

The sheriff got around to back of the house, picked the lock and walked in slowly. As he entered the kitchen he heard pounding coming from the attic. He opened the door and slowly walked up the stairs to the attic. He reached and door and could hear Swans swearing at Sarah.

"It's not here, you lied to me."
"No I didn't, I swear that's where my dad told me he put it."
"I warned your father that I would kill you if I didn't get my money."
"Swans, let her go. There is no way out."

Swans grabbed Sarah from behind and quickly drew a gun to her head.

"Back up or I will kill her."
"Drop the gun Swans. We have the whole place surrounded. There is no place for you to run."
"I said back up or I will kill her."
"Sarah, are you okay?"
"John, is that you?"
"I'm here Sarah."
"I thought I told you to stay in the car?"

"It looks like you need my help now."
"Just stay out of the way."
"Shut up and back away or I'll drop her like a dog."
"Swans think about it, if you hurt her you're going to die."
"Then take me out."
"Let her go. It doesn't have to come to this."
"All I want is what coming to me and I'll leave."
"That's not an option."
"Do you want me to kill her?"
"You're not leaving me with any options. Let the girl go or you're going to die."
"I can't and you know that."

Sarah knew she needed to get away and she needed to find her opportunity.

"Were going to back up slowly and when I reach the door I will let her go."
"Don't move Swans."
"I said I would let her go."
"We can't let you go, you know that."

Sarah could feel the sweat from Swans soaking her back. She needed to get away from him some how.

"Swans, let her go or I'm going to have to shoot you."
"You're going to shoot me either way, so I might as well take her out with me."
"You don't want to do that Swans."
"You're not leaving me any options."
"Let her go and we can talk about it."

Swans raised the gun to Sarah head and she began to cry. The sheriff knew he had to take his shot. Sarah could feel the wind from the bullet an it passed by her face. Swans grip loosened from around her neck as he fell to the floor.

"Sarah, are you okay?"

"John, hold me please."

"I'm here Sarah. I'm here and you're safe now."

"How did you get out of prison?"

"That's a long story and I think Devon should be the one to tell you."

"I don't want to talk to him."

"Sarah, just relax. Let's get in the car and take you to the emergency room, your head is bleeding."

"I want to know what's going on."

"You will Sarah, I promise."

Sarah sat quietly wrapped in only John's coat wrapped in his arms as they road to the hospital.

Devon arrived at the hospital with a look of fear in his eyes.

"Where is Sarah? Is she okay?"

"She's fine Devon, but she is really angry at you. Remember she still thinks that you killed her parents."

"How am I going to tell her the truth?"

"You will find a way. She has the right to know the truth and you are the one she has to hear it from."

Devon walked through the door to Sarah's room and hung his head in shame.

"What are you doing here? Shouldn't you be in jail?"

"Sarah, you need to listen to me."

"I don't want to listen to you."

"You have to Sarah, I didn't kill your parents and I didn't do what you think I did."

"Then who is responsible for all of this?"

"Are you sure you can handle this?"

"You are joking right. After everything I've been through you have the guts to ask me that."

"Sarah, this is very hard for me to say."

"Just say it before I have you thrown out of here."

"Sarah, it was your father who was on the take. It was your father who killed John's father and he also killed your mother."

"I'm not listening to this."

"Sarah, you have to believe me. I couldn't let you find out the truth that's why I told you that they had been robbed. I was doing an audit when I realized what was going on. Your father was stealing insurance money and using my social security number. He had set up a whole new identity. I never wanted you to find out the truth. I know how much your father meant to you."

"Why are you lying to me?"

"Sarah, I'm sorry. I never wanted you to learn the truth."

"You're not telling me the truth."

"Ask the Sheriff. He will tell you. He was there with me the night your parents died. He knows what really happened."

"I'm supposed to believe you and the sheriff? What kind of idiot do you think I am? All the two have done is tried to ruin my life."

"Sarah, you have to believe me. I would never lie to you about this!"

"Devon, if what you're telling me is the truth then why did the sheriff arrest John for having the gun that killed my parents?"

"I can't believe after all this time you have no idea?"

"I don't have the patience for this Devon, what are you talking about?"

"I'm in love with you Sarah and I knew you were falling in love with John. I thought if we got him convicted for killing your parents you would run to me."

Sarah couldn't believe what Devon was telling her.

"Devon, if you really loved me you would have never done any of this."

"All I did was try and protect you from the truth."

"The truth. Do you even know what the truth is anymore?"

"Sarah, I'm sorry I put you through all this."

"If my father really did this, what happened to all the money he stole?"

"We traced it to a bank account in California. We think he was ready to run. We found fake identification in his safety deposit box. He was prepared to set up a whole new life."

"Why did he kill my mother?"

"I don't know Sarah. I think he tried to convince her to come with him and she wouldn't have anything to do with it."

The tears began to well up in her eyes at what Devon was telling her. How could this be happening?

"Why Devon. Why did he have to do it?"

"I don't know Sarah. We may never understand. I'm sorry that I lied to you."

"I don't think I will ever trust you again."

"I hope someday you will."

John opened the door and saw Sarah's eyes filled with tears. He still only had one goal in life and that was to protect Sarah

"Can I come in?"

"Yeah, I think were done here. I'll wait outside. By the way John, I guess I owe you an apology too. I hope you can at least try to understand why I did it?"

"I don't think I will ever understand what you were thinking Devon."

"Are you going to press charges against us? It would be totally understandable if you were."

"I haven't decided yet."

"I understand, I'll leave you two alone now."

John walked over to Sarah and reached out for her hand.

"John, I'm so sorry for what we have all put you through. What are we going to do now?"

"You're going to heal and I'm going to help you."

"How can you even look at me knowing what my father did to you? Besides what the sheriff and Devon tried to do to you."

"The same way I looked at you before. Sarah, I love you, that hasn't changed."

"Will this ever be over for us?"

"It is over Sarah."

"I wish I was as sure as you are."

"We have our whole life in front of us. I made a promise to you; do you remember?"

"Yes, I remember."

"I want you to get better so I can make good on my promise."

"It might take me some time John."

"That's okay, all we have is time. I'm not going anywhere."

"I love you John."

"I love you too, Sarah."

Printed in the United States
20235LVS00002B/55-102